HOT LOVE INFERNO

Prophecy Allocation Series Book Two

NICKY BLUE

CONTENTS

START HERE

Hi! Thanks for buying my book. Please strap yourself in and prepare for the ride. I'll try and get around to all of you with soft drinks and light snacks.

If you'd like to know more about me, and why I'm dressed up as Gary Numan above. Please visit my Amazon profile by going to the link below:

http://viewauthor.at/nickyblue

One last thing, If you guess who the narrator of this book is by chapter 10 you win a prize. A candlelit dinner with one of the galaxies leading scientific minds. On the menu will be the most scrumptious shepherds pie you could ever imagine.

Chapter One

AN APOCRYPHAL TALE

The year was 1995, and it was a sunny March morning in Portslade. The gates of the level crossing beeped as they opened to let a passing train into the bustling city of Brighton, where the rich people lived. Robbie the hairdresser put his advertising board onto the pavement, while elderly ladies bartered joie de vivre in the post office queue next door. Across the street, charity shop volunteers sorted through bags of donations, putting the best bits aside for themselves before opening for business.

Robbie tutted at the steady stream of urinal cake flowing down the gutter from the blocked public toilets outside the train station. *Someone should lose their job over that.*

Intending to call the council, he turned to go back into his shop, but got distracted by Merril, who was bending over to pick up her bus pass. All along the high street, buskers and street vendors competed with the ceaseless roar of roadworks for attention.

A five minute walk south from the hairdressers was the jetty, where the early morning fog continued to thin, leaving only a faint haze behind it and revealing a squadron of seagulls hovering like stealth bombers high in the emerging blue above as they awaited the return of the fishing trawlers. Curtains were being pulled back, shutters were opening, and pots of tea were being poured as the façade of ordinary life played itself out for yet another day.[1]

Up above the town, on the edges of the craggy chalk cliffs, three dark and war-torn figures stepped out of the fog. Their leader removed his horned helmet and spat ectoplasm into the cool salty breeze. Drawing his sword, he screamed the words, 'Sambō-Kōjin' as he pointed towards a patch of land at the edge of the town; the Portslade Allotments.[2]

For nature lovers, this was the perfect time of the year; the terror of winter now a fading memory, the daffodils poking their heads up, ushering in nine months of peace and solitude in the great outdoors. That is, if you weren't having your eardrums assaulted by Brian Fowler.

Barry Harris was beginning to realise why his had been the only application to the local council for this rather neglected plot.

'Have you heard of the legend of Mrs Jittery Twitch?' asked Brian, putting down his can of herbicide and leaning on the fence that separated their allotments.

'No,' replied Barry, wondering wearily if this was some kind of joke.

'She used to be a familiar part of local folklore, but people dare not talk about her anymore, and no one really knows if she exists. Some say she's half woman, half cockroach, and came into being when the two were fused in a bizarre gardening accident. Others say she's a mutated demon sent from the hell realms to punish the wicked.'

'Really?' Barry's eyes widened sarcastically as he sat on an upside down bucket, forgetting about his work.

'She lives in the corners of reality, watching us. She knows our shadow sides intimately, and feeds on the hate of our enemies.'

The colour started to drain from Barry's face, so he looked down and scratched at the dirt with a twig to hide it from Brian. 'What does she look like?' he asked, trying to make it sound like he didn't really care.

'It's said she has five hundred arms and burning eyes that can melt your brain just by looking at you. She wears thick dark glasses, and only takes them off when she decides punishment is justified.'

'Shit!' Barry fumbled with his flask to reassure himself, twisting the top off clumsily. 'How do we know she's not just a fairy tale?'

Brian took a handkerchief from his pocket and wiped the back of his neck. He'd snared his audience, and knew the value of a dramatic pause. He continued slowly.

'There is...a way...to summon her, but only if you need help fighting your enemies.'

'How?' asked Barry, now hanging on Brian's every word.

'Listen, this isn't something you want to know about, and I don't even know if it works. No one dares beckon her, because they will be forever in her debt if they do. If she came calling for you in the future, you might have to perform unspeakable acts on her behalf.'

Barry had fallen for Brian's favourite trick—get 'em keen then treat 'em mean— and he hated not knowing. He was one of those people that had to see the end of a movie no matter how dreadful it was. 'Just tell me!' His nostrils started to flare.

'Alright, since you've forced my hand. Are you really sure you want to know? I *have* warned you...'

Barry's face began its rapid, well-known transformation into purple, making Brian chuckle.

'Calm down, old man, I will tell you. You simply have to recite the following incantation out loud.' Brian fetched a pen from his shed and scribbled away on the back of his yearly planting calendar. 'Just look at it, don't even read it in your mind.'

Are you a devil? Are you a witch? Judge the soul of my enemies, Mrs Jittery Twitch.

Barry looked at the words, his heart clattering against his ribcage. Taking a deep breath, he turned back to Brian.

'What would happen next if I said it out loud?'

'She appears out of nowhere and asks a question of such significance that, when your enemies answer,[3] she learns everything she needs to make her judgement.'

'Judgement? What judgement?' Barry threw his hands in the air, bewildered.

'Ah!' Brian grew histrionic, delighted his new neighbour was so easy. 'But if Jittery's judgment doesn't fall in their favour—'

'Tell me!'

'She gets very twitchy.'

'That's terrifying,' replied Barry, dropping his shoulders so his hands came to rest on his knees. 'I see that every time my mum misses her medication.'

Brian edged closer to Barry and looked him in the eye. 'This is no joking matter. The *real* problems start when she gets twitchy. If she decides your enemies deserve a quick death, she takes her glasses off, and the next thing you know, their brains are dribbling out of their noses. If, however, she decides your antagonist warrants a sterner penalty, she works herself up into such an animated frenzy that she explodes, reducing the soul of your enemy...to dust. After that, no one will hear from her again until she is reborn from the sins of future generations.'

Silent as a snowflake, Barry stared down at the dregs of his tomato soup. He looked up at Brian, puffed up his cheeks, and blew out a long stream of air as he clambered to his feet.

'That's definitely a punishment if I ever heard of one. I wouldn't ever need to call on her of course, not with my ninjutsu training. I'm a walking weapon of mass destruction.' Barry started a punch sequence to show off his skills.

Brian took a few steps backwards and covered his mouth while he cleared his throat, trying to make his laughter look like a coughing fit.

'I'll be sure not to upset you then, old chap! Is there any more news about your dad and Mindy?'

Barry stared wistfully out over the allotments for a few moments before replying.

'The police found a picture of a Japanese model in dad's underwear drawer, so they reckon he's gone off with her and taken Mindy with him. They've closed the case. Something doesn't add up about it though, something's not right.'

'Don't talk to me about the bloody police! I reported Arthur at plot 67 for selling cannabis from his shed, and they've done nothing, even though it completely contravenes allotment policy. He says it's for medicinal use, but he keeps falling over whilst trying to turn his compost. He's totally off his tits.'[4]

Ending a conversation with Brian was a bit like trying to get rid of bindweed; virtually impossible. Apart from his obsession with weeds, allotment policy, and fairy tales, he could speak on any subject without stopping for hours, possibly days. He could even dispense with the need for breathing when he really got into a flow.

By the time Barry got home, it was almost nightfall. He took some fish fingers out of the freezer and walked over to the window to close the curtains. It was be a misty night, though he could still see his neighbour's old Basset Hound staring up at him from their back garden. Barry instantly felt uneasy, but didn't know why. He pulled the curtains closed for a few moments, then opened them again to find the hound was still gawking at him. Its expression seemed irritated, like it was pissed off about something. Barry closed the curtains again and waited long enough for condensation to form on the box of defrosting fish in his hand before carefully peeling the bottom corner of the curtain up so he could peer out without being seen. This time, the hound seemed to be raising its eyebrows, as if to say, 'really?'

Sarcastic bastard! thought Barry. *Sod this, fish fingers and then bed.*

---

1. To this day, you won't find designer clothing outlets or artisan coffee shops here; but what you may find will force you to question the very nature of existence. If you wait long enough on any street corner in Portslade, sooner or later a crack in the fabric of reality might appear. This story takes you inside one of those cracks. There are those who would tell you that this tale is far too fantastic to be true, but what I would say in reply is that even if you don't believe that the following events happened, it does not make them any less real. I'm your narrator, by the way, the same person that's telling the story above, but I tend to express myself a bit more via the medium of footnotes. It's my job to help you decipher the odd piece of British vernacular used throughout this book. I will also be offering commentary on the story as we go, but I need to have on record that it is not my role to state whether this

story did or did not happen. My job is to present the facts as I know them, in all their squalid and debauched detail. This journey is not for the faint-hearted; you have been warned.

2. An allotment is a field that the council allows older men and women to retreat to with flasks of soup to read the newspaper and maybe do a spot of gardening. After an allotment has been running for about ten years, the council kick everybody off the land in order to build affordable housing, which, mysteriously, no one can ever afford.

3. And you can't stop yourself from answering.

4. 'Off your tits' means to be intoxicated on drink or drugs, and can be substituted for 'off your head'. I'm not sure how the tits found their way into this variation. Like Barry, I am a feminist; part of my job description has been to study feminism and psychoanalysis, which I have found fascinating. I was particularly drawn to the French writer Hélène Cixous and her notion of 'the great arm of parental-conjugal phallocentrism'. I felt less affinity, however, with the 1960s radical feminist group SCUM (Society for Cutting Up Men) for some reason, not that their philosophy applies to me in any way.

Chapter Two

THE MIST

Clothed head to foot in urban camouflage, Barry spun round and pelted a ninja star with all his force. Its deadly razor-sharp blades whistled as they cut through the air. The power and precision of a weapon like this was an awesome spectacle to behold, and that made it the killing tool of choice for some of history's most feared ninjas. There is a tale that an entire samurai army was defeated by a group of ninja fighters using such a weapon. On this occasion, however, it completely missed the dartboard and stuck into the wall.

'Are you throwing those spikey things again?' screamed Molly from down the hallway.

'No, Mum, I dropped something.'

'You'll be moving into the garden shed if you are! Get in here now.'

'Coming.'

Barry was a not-very-tall, portly man of twenty-eight with irritable bowel syndrome and an insatiable appetite for fish fingers, and the last two of these distinguishing features may have been related. He shared a studio flat above the Astral

Waves Hair Salon with Molly, his dear mother, who at sixty had an equal love for boiled sweets and death metal bands. These were almost certainly unrelated. Molly had been known to get through ten packets of pear drops in a day until her dentist warned her she was in danger of rotting her teeth. She had tried to quit, and was doing well until her bingo team won a gallon jar of whiskey-and-cola flavoured humbugs. The temptation proved just too strong, and she was back on them in no time.

Three years ago, Barry's sister Mindy and his Japanese father Yamoshi had gone out shopping and never returned home. As far as Barry was concerned, the police investigation had been worse than useless; having concluded with no concrete evidence. Both he and his mother felt like they had been left in limbo without answers and with no possible relief on the horizon. The trauma was so severe for Molly that the only way she could keep herself afloat was with a cocktail of antidepressants and ear-splitting death metal. She tried to put on a brave face for Barry's sake, but he had come to gauge the darkness of Molly's mood by the intensity of music she was listening to. Motörhead, for example, was the mark of an average morning, often accompanied by pancakes. A song from Abominable Putridity, however, was an indicator for Barry to get off to work early. Being the oldest metal-head in Portslade, Molly longed to find someone to go to gigs with. Barry would have offered, but he had the sneaking suspicion the music exacerbated his IBS.

Barry sat down on one of the old plastic kitchen chairs and let out a yelp. Molly had bought them as a job lot from Greek Trevor, who owned the chip shop in the high street. She liked them because they looked retro, and were, ironically, cheap as chips.

'These things have been ripping lumps out of my arse for years!' cried Barry.

'How many times do have I have to tell you? Put two seats together, one bum-cheek on each, and you'll be fine,' his mother said smoothly. No one could get up early enough to catch Molly out.

The kitchen was vibrating with all manner of electrical whirring, beeping and buzzing, and Barry's nostrils were assaulted by a heady mix of raw onions, burning pasta, microwave popcorn, and pine floor cleaner. Condensation dribbled down the walls and visibility had been greatly reduced by the mass of steam collecting into a fog in the centre of the room. They couldn't afford to fix the extractor fan, and Molly thought it still far too cold to open the window. She hunched over some bubbling pots in the corner like a witch over her cauldron, cooking up a tuna casserole from a recipe she'd heard on the radio. Barry scraped the mould off some crusts (all that remained of a white sliced loaf) and reached over to pop them in the toaster. Beads of condensation dripped down the appliance—if its frayed wires weren't caked in layers of cooking fat, it would almost certainly have been a fire hazard. He then joined in with the electrical orchestra by slurping Ribena through a novelty straw, the spirally kind that is great fun to use but brings on mild hyperventilation. He picked up Molly's scribbled recipe list, certain she'd not remembered all the ingredients correctly.

A new (but equally pungent) odour started burning the lining of Barry's nasal cavities, reminding him of new tennis balls. It was accompanied by a rotten egg sulphuric taste that registered deep in the back of his throat. Growing increasingly concerned about what approached him through the mist, Barry fingered the word '*HELP*' into the spilt sugar granules on the kitchen tabletop. Should they both be found dead sometime in the future—immaculately preserved like the people of Pompeii—they may at least be able to trace the cause of death.

'I've had to improvise a bit.' Molly dumped a lump of luminous orange gunge onto Barry's plate.

'I didn't have any tuna, so I had to use your fish fingers and a few old tins from the cupboard. I'm not sure what they were, the labels had fallen off. It's all food though in't it?'

'I'm sure it will be lovely, Mum,' replied Barry, thankful for the steam camouflage as he poked at the entity with a fork. As soon as Molly turned her back, he picked the creation up and dumped it in the only place he could think of; the pocket of the work jacket draped on the back of his chair. He turned back to find Molly standing over him, wafting the steam out of her face.

'You look like you're enjoying that, here have some more.' She dumped a double helping onto his plate, then sat down to join the feast.

'Cor, this is delicious, in't it!' Molly gulped down huge mouthfuls like a great pelican feasting on carp.

'I'm not sure I can manage much more, Mum, I'm feeling stuffed.' Barry made a big show of rubbing his stomach to display his satisfaction.

'Nonsense, I've made loads, get it down you,' said Molly, giving him a luminous smile.

Yamoshi, being from Japan, used to regale Barry with stories about the ways samurai would assassinate their enemies. Food poisoning was among the most common and hardest to guard against. He used to joke that if Barry could survive 20 years of Molly's cooking, it wasn't something he needed to worry about. Nibbling gingerly at the edge of the orange blob on his fork, Barry felt a tingling in the nerves of his teeth.

What the hell is in this?

Sensing Molly was looking at him, and seeing no way out

of his quandary, he bit down hard on the charcoal-encrusted morsel, almost dislodging a filling in the process.

'Ouch!' Barry grabbed the side of his mouth.

'You alright, love? I probably shouldn't have left it in for so long.' As the steam started to clear, Molly looked closer at the contents of her plate. 'It's a bit shiny too, in't it? Think I over did it with the food colouring.' Molly pointed to a half empty packet next to the cooker. 'They said on the radio it's got something called 'castoreum' in it that makes it orange, apparently.'

'Never heard of it,' said Barry, simultaneously chewing, smiling ,and trying not to swallow.

'They don't ever list it in the ingredients because of what it is.'

If it were possible for Barry to show any more concern, he managed it. 'What would that be?'

'The anal gland juice from a Eurasian beaver.'[1]

Barry spat the contents of his mouth across the kitchen table.

'It's no different from eating eggs, you know!' Molly wiped her mouth with a dirty tea towel. 'Well, *I* enjoyed that, even if no one else did! It's good to test yourself every now and then.'

'I think you managed that, Mum.' Barry looked down at his glimmering pocket—if he was more paranoid, he would've been certain it had just winked at him.

Carrying a packet of biscuits and a bowl of popcorn, they both took the short walk to the front room.

'Do you mind if I play a bit of Metallica?' Molly called as she took a CD out of its case. 'This reminds me of her so much.' Mindy had been the original metal fan of the family and although Molly had complained bitterly when she had first started blaring it, it was now the closest link she had to her daughter. 'Have you seen the state of that new hairdresser downstairs, Robbie something or other? He looks like a cross between a wizard and a bull mastiff. Merril swears he tried to touch her arse when she was in there the other day, I'm not letting him near my barnet.'[2]

'He sounds like a gentleman,' said Barry, shaking his head. ' At least he's fixed the overhead hairdryers so you won't have to drip dry anymore.'

'I went to look at another hairdresser's in Hove yesterday,' said Molly, 'but they charge about five times as much as downstairs and you have to have soya milk in your tea. I'd prefer to suck on a dirty nappy.'

Barry opened the biscuits and flopped down next to his mum on the old lumpy futon that—much to his displeasure— doubled as his bed.

'You'll have to kip[3] in my bed tonight darling, I'll be up late with a video Ril lent me.'

Considering their ongoing hardship and cramped living space, the only real argument between himself and Molly had been over a saucy Charlie Dimmock[4] poster Barry wanted to put up in the kitchen. Molly objected, complaining that she didn't want to have to look at Charlie's boobs when eating her morning porridge. Barry resigned himself to putting it up in the toilet (where it still resides to this day) placing it at just the right height for Molly to write possible crossword answers on whilst performing her morning ablutions.

'Mum, you know that Basset Hound in the butcher's garden?'

'Yes, dear?'

'Every time I look out of the kitchen window, he's staring up at me.'

'Poor thing is bored out of his little mind, I expect. I've never seen them take him for a walk once.'

'He's got a huge garden to play in, but he just sits on that step and stares up at our window, it's stressing me out.' Barry found himself slumping further down in his seat, wedging his head between two large bumps in the futon. Molly had turned the central heating up so high it sent him into a bit of a stupor, and he found himself drifting back to his school days.

Growing up in Portslade in the 1970s had been a tough bit of business. When a boy left school, he had the choice of two very clearly defined career paths; the steel yard or the dole office. By not taking up one of these revered vocational pathways, you risked being ostracised and even having your masculinity questioned by the town's menfolk. Barry had thought long and hard about it, spending many nights chatting through his options with Molly. In the end, he opted for a career in horticulture, the primary reason for his decision being that it would take him as far away as possible from the people who became steel-workers or dole-boys.[5] Barry had been bullied by them his whole life.

'Just ignore him, he's a dog.' said Molly, jolting Barry upright and bringing him back to the conversation. He got the same feeling of judgement from that bloody dog, even if it could never *actually* bully him.

'He's got a really annoying face,' said Barry

'You should hear what he says about you!' Molly chuckled. As Barry joined in her laughter, Molly seized the opportunity to squeeze a sensitive agenda into the conversation. 'Have you thought any more about getting out and doing some dating?'

'Not this again, Mum.' Barry reached over and stole some of Molly's popcorn.

'I worry about you, is all! You must get lonely being on your own all the time.'

'I'm fine. I'm still recovering from Amanda Jowers.'

'You were fifteen.'

'It was true love—'

'It was anything but!' Molly began picking the remains of

casserole out of her teeth with a bit of rolled-up biscuit wrapper.

'Truth is, Mum, I'm a bit...' Barry avoided Molly's eyes.

'Yes, dear?'

'...tired. I'm off to bed. Night.'

'Night, dear,' sighed Molly, putting her feet up and cracking open a can of Special Brew. She didn't drink it very often as it made her poo funny, but Merril had lent her all six seasons of *Xena: Warrior Princess* on VHS, and this was going to be one hell of an all-nighter.

---

1. That's considered a delicacy where I come from!
2. Cockney rhyming slang meaning 'hair'. The long form is 'Barnet Fair' which was a horse festival in North London circa 1758. I used to enjoy going, and it has a special place in my heart as it's where I met my wife. It's a shame she turned into a bit of a nag! (If you don't find my footnote jokes funny, please keep in mind that they're part of the 50% extra free gags the advertising refers to. You aren't being charged for them.)
3. Kip means to sleep.
4. Charlie Dimmock is a TV presenter and gardening expert. She is well known for not wearing a bra whilst gardening, which makes her the horticultural equivalent of Pamela Anderson. Barry thinks about her every day.
5. Dole-boy – A man that lives on financial benefits provided by the state without any intention of entering into gainful employment. There is definitely something to be said for it as a vocation; you get to lounge around in your underwear watching Scooby Doo and smoking weed all day at the expense of the taxpayer. The British government have been trying to modernise the benefits system so anyone capable of employment should be made to work, but such Draconian measures are bound to fail.

Chapter Three

BURN YOUR BRA

M olly had been irritated by a lump in the side of her armchair for months. Fearing the lining had gone blobby, she had avoided looking at it as she didn't want to pay to have it reupholstered. When she eventually got around to conducting a deeper investigation, however, she discovered it was actually the video of *Four Weddings and a Funeral* she had rented from the Blockbuster. Being a beacon of responsibility, she ascribed her son the job of shoving the film into the shop's letterbox without being seen. In doing so, Molly would escape the five-pound fine that could have seriously dented her boiled sweet budget. It being a Sunday, the shop would be closed, and so it was the perfect time for such a stealth mission.

Compared to some of the treacherous undercover operations Barry had allegedly undertaken in the past, this was—as they say—a walk in the park. As the light quickly drained from the sky, it was the park that Barry now found himself in, taking a shortcut home. Missing the beginning of *Star Trek: Voyager* was simply unacceptable.[1] Arriving at the boating lake, Barry noticed it was unusually quiet for a weekend afternoon.

Is there a fair on in town, maybe?

He made his way towards the entrance to the woods just as a dense fog descended. It hit the ground in waves, edging towards him. He ran into the woods for cover, but it followed him, worming between the trees like tentacles.

What the...?

Barry's thought was cut off and replaced by fear as the outline of a tall dark figure emerged from the fog and began running towards him. The moonlight illuminated two bloodied bullhorns on its hat as it began slicing the air with a vast steel blade. Barry sprinted faster than he ever had before, skipping over fallen branches and dodging ditches in the failing light. Out of the corner of his eye, he could see the figure gaining ground on him. The fog was encasing him, but if he strained he could just make out a faint light in the distance.

Is it a streetlight?

The rough bark of the conifer trees tore at Barry's arms as he collided into them. He had to keep going...

He ran faster and faster until...*bang!* He hit something hard that sent him down onto the moist tarmac with a dull thud.

The bright haze of a streetlight fizzled around the edges of Barry's consciousness as the overpowering scent of pipe smoke pervaded his awareness.

'Barry, can you hear me?'

'Huh?'

'It's Dr Harper. Speak to me, boy.'

'Wha'...happened?' Barry rubbed his forehead.

'You came tearing out of the woods and straight into me,' said the doctor.

Barry quickly turned his head towards the trees. 'There was someone chasing me...'

'No, it was just you.'

'You sure?'

'Sit up, boy, have some tea.' The doctor handed him a warm flask.

Barry propped himself up against the street light and stared back into the wood. It was deserted, with no fog or horned shadow creature in sight.

'How's the stress been, Barry? Remember the option for medication we spoke about?'

'I'm fine, I just...maybe I've been overdoing it lately.'

'You do lead an exciting life. What I would give to swap with you, just for a day!' The doctor stared intently into his eyes.

Barry glanced down at his watch. Grabbing hold of the doctor, he abruptly pulled himself to his feet. 'I'm going to miss Star Trek.'

'Before you go, Barry, I've been given these paging devices. They are supposed to be for patient emergencies, but no one knows how to use them.' He thrust a chunky black gadget into Barry's reluctant hand. 'If you ever need me, day or night, just buzz me and I'll be there to support you. We can be like the dynamic duo!' The doctor's face lit up at the possibility of untold exotic adventures.[2]

By the time Barry got home, it was half-past five, leaving him ten minutes to shower, shave, eat six fish fingers and explain to Molly why his arms were the colour of rhubarb. It would be tight, but his austere training had prepared him for exactly this kind of eventuality.

'I'm sure I saw someone in the woods,' Barry said as he rammed two fish fingers into his gullet.

'It wasn't the manager of Blockbusters, was it?' said Molly, placing a bowl of runny Angel Delight[3] onto the coffee table.

'With a sword and a horned hat?'

'He's a bit of a jobsworth.'[4] Molly nodded at the possibility.

Barry plopped his sweaty feet down on the coffee table and slurped at his Angel Delight just as the Star Trek theme tune started. Precision timing of this calibre was a thing of rare beauty.

Knowing Barry would be at home, Molly had invited her best mate Merril round for a cup of tea and to help her orchestrate a rather cunning plan.

Bing Bong!

'Who the bloody hell is that?' Barry asked, bright pink mousse dribbling down the side of his chin.

'It's only Ril, we won't bother you.'

'You better not.'

To this day, Merril has her own key to the flat, but always rings the doorbell to give advance warning of her arrival. Around five minutes later, she appears at the top of the stairs and glides into the front room.[5]

As she entered, Molly greeted her friend with a hug. 'You sit in the armchair, I'll put the kettle on.'

'Ta love, my feet are killing me.'

'What do you think of Star Trek, Ril?' Molly shouted from the kitchen.

'I would,' said Merril, pointing at Commander Chakotay.

'You saucy git! I love a man in a uniform too,' said Molly, bringing in a bowl of whiskey-and-cola humbugs.

'Can you two be quiet if you're going to stay in here?'

'Don't worry,' said Merril, 'we'll be like little mice. Just fill me in the story, will ya love?'

Barry tutted, 'There's an alien race called called Vidiians that harvest people's organs, and they've stolen the lungs of one of the Voyager's crew members called Neelix.'

'They'd be welcome to my lungs, I keep hocking up these

phlegm gems... something's not right.'

Barry edged his way to the other side of the futon, closer to the television, adopting a posture of committed concentration.

Molly plonked herself down next to him.

'Ril, I've been telling Barry to stop messing around with all this ninja business and get himself a girlfriend.'

'That's a good idea, love,' said Merril.

Barry stayed transfixed on the screen as

Molly looked over at Merril and gave her a wink.

'I could fix you up on a date with my niece Joanna Tarry, she's been single for weeks now,' bleated Merril on cue.

'No way!' Barry wagged his index finger, keeping focused on the screen. 'She used to ignore me at school. I'm not bloody desperate.'

'Jo is *lovely*,' said Molly, narrowing her eyes.

'I'm sure she is, but what are the chances of us having anything in common? Rumi says the only way we can find love is to undo the barriers we have built up against it.'

Molly and Merril stared at Barry for a few moments before looking at each other and giggling.

'The only barrier you have,' said Molly, 'is having no one to get your leg over with!'

'You two don't take anything seriously.' Barry dug himself deeper into the futon, trying to catch up on what Trekkie action he'd missed.[6]

Merril, deciding to take some initiative, shuffled onto the edge of the futon next to Molly and reached over to put her hand on Barry's leg.

'That's not true, darling. Your mum is worried about you is all, she wants you to be 'appy. I've told Jo all about what you're up to these days, and she told me to tell you she's been to see the Teenage Mutant Ninja Turtle film, so you would have that in common.'

'That's great.' Barry rolled his eyes skyward.

'How's her epilepsy been?' asked Molly.

'She's been having a terrible time with it to be honest. She was having these dreadful seizures, I thought I was gunna lose her at one point. They've got her on this new medication now, and as long as she keeps taking it she'll be OK.'

'The poor love! You see, you'd be really cheering her up by taking her out.' Molly fluttered her eyelashes at Barry.

'I'm not a carer, and there is absolutely no way in a million years that I am going on a date with her! Now can I watch Star Trek, PLEASE?' Barry picked up his Rumi book and threw it across the room, causing to it to rebound off the mini bar and land a rubber plant that should have been repotted years ago. It had become increasingly difficult to control his temper since his father had gone missing; it was as though a primal beast seemed to take him over at times. He took some deep breaths to collect himself, and as he calmed down, the room was silent. Molly and Merril were surveying the floor, as if suddenly interested in the dust bunnies under the coffee table. Eventually, Molly stood up and offered around a tray of chocolate digestives.

'She's got massive tits, Barry.'

'You're not wrong there,' said Merril. 'They're like a pair of space hoppers; I don't know how she walks upright. She's had one of those boob tubes done.'

'She means boob *job*,' Molly grinned.

'Yes, that's the one,' said Merril, pointing at Molly. 'She had to save up for a year for it, she's only on minimum wage at the Factory.'

Barry shook his head, picked up a copy of *The Female Eunuch* from the coffee table and waved it in the air. 'This is just demeaning, you know I'm a feminist. I wonder what Germaine Greer would have to say to you two?'

An awkward stalemate followed as Molly annoyed Barry

by kicking at the frayed edges of her rag rug, and Barry annoyed Molly by watching Star Trek. Merril annoyed everyone by slowly cracking all her knuckles, one by one.

Eventually, Merril broke the silence.

'I don't know why you're getting so touchy, me and your mum are feminists, aren't we Mol?'

Molly nodded tentatively, wondering where this was going.

'And if anyone knows about feminism, it's me. I'm a woman.'

'I hadn't noticed,' replied Barry dryly.

'Mol, tell him what I did when that bloke refused to give his seat up for me on the bus to Brighton.'

'You grabbed hold of his gonads.'

'Yeah, and squeezed 'em till he fainted.'

'It was a pity you hadn't seen his wheelchair though, Ril.'

'It was folded up! Anyway, the point is, I don't put up with any mischief from men.'

'I don't know why Simone de Beauvoir bothered writing *The Second Sex*,' said Barry, shaking his head again and chomping on a digestive biscuit. 'Look, if you're both going to make a big fuss about it and it will shut you up, I don't suppose it would hurt to go.'

Molly looked over at her accomplice and rolled her eyes with delight.

'Fantastic.' said Merril. 'What about tomorrow night? I know Jo's got nuffin' on. Why don't you take her to the pictures?'

'To-tomorrow? That soon?'

'That's sorted then,' said Merril, 'I'll tell her to meet you outside the Goat and Ferret pub at 7pm.'

Barry nodded, burrowing himself into the futon like a sand crab. A sense of impending doom appeared in the pit of his stomach, forcing him to forget about whether Neelix would ever get his lungs back, and go in search of some Victoria sponge.[7] No sooner had he opened the larder door than the phone started ringing.

'Hello?'

'Ah, Mr Harris, it's Mrs Caswell from the Bowls Academy. I'm just calling to confirm our appointment this Wednesday. As you know, we have a coach-load coming over from Shoreham for the big game on Friday.'

'Yes, I haven't forgotten,' replied Barry, irritated by the Sunday evening intrusion.

'Need I remind you, Mr Harris, that you didn't turn up last time and left us completely in the lurch—'

'I have already apologised for that, Mrs Caswell, it was a personal matter and was completely out of my control.'[8]

'Be that as it may, the regional semi-finals are this Saturday, so the green will need that extra bit of magic.'

Barry groaned under his breath.

'It will need cutting, aerating, treating, and rolling—twice,' said Mrs Caswell.

'Twice? That will take me all day, and I put my back out using that roller! Is it really necessary?'

Mrs Caswell let out a deep sigh directly into the phone receiver.

'Mr Harris, I don't think you fully understand our situation. This is the first time The Portslade Premier Bowls Academy have made it this far in a tournament; we have never hosted an event of this magnitude. There will be hell to pay if we don't get the correct camber on the green, and we're counting on you not to let us down. Anyway, it's too short notice to get anyone else, so we don't have any other option.'

'You could just tarmac the whole green and play skittles instead,' Barry quipped.

'I'm warning you, Mr Harris. If there is one blade of grass

out of place, the trustees will be informed, and you don't want to be on the wrong side of *them*.'

'They are all in their eighties! What are they going to do, write me a stern letter, if they can do that without getting a collective hernia?'

'Don't take that tone with me, Mr—'

'Sod off!' Barry threw the phone out of the open kitchen window, narrowly missing the Bassett Hound, who was still staring blankly up at him.

'And you can sod off as well!'

---

1. Barry wasn't a massive sci-fi fan, but he did have a bit of a man (or Vulcan) crush on Spock. There was something about his ethereal presence and the fact he was so in control. Barry would experience an extremely high dopamine rush when Spock used his Vulcan nerve pinch in particular, whereas I can't see what the fuss is about; I've invented at least thirty-five that are just as deadly.

2. Little did the doctor realise that even his most twisted nightmares could not prepare him for how exotic those adventures would become, and trust me when I tell you his nightmares are pretty damn twisted.

3. Angel Delight is a powdered packet dessert you mix with milk to form a mousse.

4. This refers to an individual who delights in being obstructive, citing their occupation's petty rules and regulations to justify their actions. You would not believe the amount of times I've been told my mere presence contravenes a health and safety policy. I'm cleaner than most humans, I'll have you know!

5. Scientists who still believe it is impossible for humans to defy the laws of gravity simply haven't met Merril. Bent double with a bipedal limp doesn't adequately express the gymnastic contortion that is her posture. She has mastered the art of limbless locomotion, having the ability to propel herself forward without using her legs. Merril navigates the world like a bizarre fusion of a hovercraft and Gollum, with a face to match.

6. It normally took all of Barry's concentration plus two or three rewatches for him to fully comprehend the storyline.

7. As far as I can tell, a Victoria sponge is pretty much the main thing Brits eat, along with curry, chips, and lager. It's a cake, by the way, and it tastes of heaven.

8. Barry had forgotten and gone up to his allotment. He has the work ethic of a dead sloth.

Chapter Four

A LITTLE SNIFTER

Barry was about to give up on the evening when he heard the clack of stilettos on concrete approaching him from behind. He turned, and there she was, standing before him like a celestial goddess...albeit one with a roll-up hanging out of her gob.[1]

In Barry's panic-stricken eyes, she was the most beautiful woman he had ever seen. The streetlights flickered off of the highlights in her hair, lacquered into place to look just like Princess Diana's. She smiled, unwittingly revealing the lipstick applied to her teeth whilst getting ready in a rush. Her black strapless dress showcased a panther tattoo she had over her right shoulder. It was obviously a work in progress; it didn't have any legs yet, and you could be forgiven for thinking it looked more like an otter. Barry's hands were shaking so much he put them in his pockets.[2]

She's changed so much...am I supposed to shake hands with her?

'Barry?'

In reply, he opened his mouth and squealed like a Klingon.

'Luvvly to meet you darlin'!'

Barry's attempt at a smile made him look constipated, and his heart was pounding so rapidly he could hardly breathe.

'The silent type, eh?'

Barry nodded, trying to look cool.

Jo's eyes were lapis blue and deep enough to lose yourself in. Life had not always been easy for her, having been kicked out of home at the age of thirteen by an alcoholic mother and forced into menial jobs to scrape by. Her health was poor, and then there were the men in her life, few of whom had ever treated her well. She couldn't help believing there were no good men left in the world, though she longed for someone to prove her wrong.

'Shall we nip in for a quick half then?' Jo pointed at the Goat and Ferret. 'It looks like you could use it.'

Barry held his thumb up and followed Jo into the pub like a lobotomised gibbon. Once inside, Barry pointed towards the gents and made a swift retreat across the threadbare spiral carpet to gather himself. He sat down on a grimy toilet seat and puffed into his paper bag—at least he had come prepared. After about five minutes, when his carbon dioxide levels had rebalanced and he was feeling marginally more human again, he made his way back to the bar. Jo had a pint of lager waiting for him on a slimy beer mat; he had never needed a drink more. He managed to offer her a big gappy grin before supping half his drink down in one gulp.

'My auntie has been telling me lots about you. She said you are a kung fu expert, like Bruce Lee?'

'A bit like that, but I'm a ninja,' replied Barry, feeling thankful his speech had returned. 'I'm probably the last one left apart from my dad...he taught me.'

'I'd love to learn a skill like that.'

'Did you know that back in Japan, ninjas would often disguise themselves as gardeners when they had to guard a palace from invaders?'

'Really?' said Jo, looking impressed.

'Yeah, no one would suspect a gardener! That's why I work as one.'

'That's interesting.' Jo rolled another cigarette with her tar-stained fingers.

'I don't tell this stuff to just anyone. I do a lot of work for the secret service; black ops, that kind of thing. I'm what's known as a prime asset, and my identity can't be revealed—there are too many lives at stake. I'd be lying if I said it wasn't a great burden, but like I say, I really can't talk about it.'

'You're like James Bond, aren't you? Tell me about one of your missions.' Jo knocked back her Martini and Tonic and signalled to the barman for another round.

'I've sworn an oath of silence.'

Jo reached over, squeezed his leg, and fluttered her eyelashes. 'Please?'

'I was on the ground in Kosovo. it was a recon mission—the British Army were too scared to get involved at that point so they flew me in to take it on. I took out an entire rebel faction and rescued around five thousand women and children. I also do land mine clearance, and I'm psychic so I know exactly where they are...but like I say I really can't talk about it.'

'If you're psychic, what colour knickers am I wearing?'

Barry's face turned fifty shades of pink. He defaulted to his only plan B: change the subject.

'So, where do you work, Jo?'

'I was out of work for ages with my health, but since they've got my meds straight I've been working as the assistant manager at the Pleasure Factory. We make sex toys and ship them all over the world.'

So much for plan B! Barry had no choice but to soldier on.

'I've had my share of health problems too,' said Barry, 'I've been getting IBS, which tends to flare up when danger is near, a bit like when Frodo Baggins' sword lights up if orcs are in the vicinity.'

'Sounds useful. I'm in charge of the dildos and strap-ons.'

'I didn't know...we had a place like that in Portslade.' Barry waved, pretending to recognize someone at the other end of the pub so he could avoid eye contact.

'It's not exactly legit, if you catch my meaning,' Jo continued, 'We're hidden away on an old industrial estate. Most places sell dildos that are between 9 and 12 inches long but all of mine are 15 inches and above, that's excluding the balls of course. I bet that would give you a run for your money?'

Barry's mind was emptier than his bank account, and all information retrieval had gone into lockdown. Plan B was initiated once again. 'Er...how much annual leave do you get?'

'Not much, but there's other perks; I get to design most of the dildos myself,' Jo grinned and winked at Barry, 'and then test them out.'

This time, Barry wasn't sure if his face had gone a fluorescent puce or had more of a late summer evening's scarlet hue. Either way, he could feel the heat from his cheeks competing with the pub's dilapidated central heating. Jo erupted into laughter and reached over the table to poke him in the ribs.

'I'm only joking! We hire that out to people.' She moved in close to whisper in Barry's ear, 'Between you and me, it's one of the ways my auntie Merril tops up her income.'

'Please stop, my brain is dissolving!' Barry covered his ears and revealed his gappy grin again.

'I got a discount on my boob job through work, what do you reckon?' said Jo, thrusting her abundant bosom in Barry's direction. Barry stared down at the ample body parts like a zombie on ketamine, his faculty of speech eluding him again.

'Boob jobs are all the rage in Hollywood.'

'We're in Portslade, though,' Barry remarked.

'Don't be a cock, you know what I mean.'

Barry turned crimson again.

'Ha ha, you're so easy to wind up.' Jo stubbed out her rollie on a soggy beer mat.

'If I'm being honest,' said Barry, 'I don't understand why women feel the need to do that to themselves. I blame the patriarchal narrative of the media.'

Jo's eyes narrowed, 'It just makes me feel better about myself, is all.'

'You shouldn't feel you need to change yourself just to get accepted by a man.'

'OK, shall I get rid of them then?'

'No, don't!...change the way you are for me.'

A wry smile swept over Jo's face.

'That's the problem with you so-called *modern men,* you come up with the right sound bites, but underneath you're all just gagging for it.'[3]

She tutted and turned to look round the pub. At the other end of the bar, two elderly women were huddled round a slot machine, complaining that it wasn't paying out whilst feeding as much money as they could into it.

Barry went quiet. He was out of his depth. Truth be known, he'd only read half of the first chapter of *The Female Eunuch,* so he decided to opt for a well-tested self-preservation tactic called 'shutting the fuck up'.[4]

'I used to go out with Graham who works at the butcher's next door to you. I think he only wanted me for you-know-what.'

A warning light in the back of Barry's mind indicated to him that he should break his self-imposed speech embargo for this.

'I want you to know, Jo, that I'm definitely not like that,' said Barry. 'I've only had one girlfriend, ever.'

He looked over at Jo to see that she wore the most radiant smile.

'How sweet is that! I think we are going to get along, you and me.'

Barry revealed his trademark grin again, this time framed by frothy lager lips. Arousing is *not* the word for that sight. 'About the butcher, there may be something you can help me with there. Have you seen the Basset Hound that sits on the back doorstep?'

'Yeah, that's Keith. He's a rescue dog; he's only had him six months. He's a funny old thing.'

'He's got a really annoying face,' said Barry, 'and he's always staring at me when I look out of the kitchen window.'

'He always seemed pissed off; he's definitely got issues.'

'Issues? What do you mean?'

'It's like he harbours resentment for people. My ex forgot to take him for a walk once, and he growls whenever he goes near him now. I'd say he's got a personality disorder; my auntie did an O-level in sociology, so I know about these things.'

'Isn't that just for humans?' said Barry, tilting his head to one side.

As Jo reached down to pick up her black PVC handbag, four large packets of tobacco spilled out onto the beer-stained carpet.

'Oops, I just picked them up from Greek Trevor, he smuggles them in from Cyprus or somewhere like that.'

'Probably Greece, hey?' said Barry smiling and raising his eyebrows.

'Yeah, probably. What time does the film start?' Jo looked over at the clock on the wall. 'It's nearly seven.'

Barry jumped up and grabbed his coat. 'Shit, we're late, come on!'

---

1. A roll-up, or rollie, is a 'roll-your-own' cigarette, a cheaper alternative to

pre-made cigarettes. I tried one once and it tasted mildly of Labrador butt. I'm a pipe smoker myself.

2. Barry had very limited experience with women. In fact, his experiences could be counted on the fingers of one hand—one *finger*, to be exact. Amanda Jowers had worked in the chip shop next to the pub on Portslade High Street when he was sixteen. She used to give Barry a free pickled onion when he went in for sausage and chips on his way home from the cinema on a Sunday evening—it took him six months to pluck up enough courage to tell her he didn't like pickled onions. Their romance blossomed silently over the chip-fat splattered fish counter until one day Barry woke up and the only thing he could think about was Amanda. He saved up his pocket money for a whole month to take her rollerblading in Brighton.

   They had the time of their lives, and Amanda told Barry she loved him on the bus home. When Barry asked if he could kiss her, she replied, 'If we can go rollerblading again next weekend.' Unfortunately, Barry fell off a ladder and broke his leg whilst trying to raise enough money by cleaning windows. While he was in hospital, Amanda wrote him a letter to say she had left him for a boy called Simon Manning, who Barry sat next to in class. Simon had a paper round and got to use his dad's scooter on weekends, so he could take her rollerblading whenever she wanted. How could Barry compete with that? His heart was completely and irrevocably broken; he had been brutalised by the fickle terrorist of love, and he believed he would never recover. You humans are so weird.

3. This means to desperately want something. It normally refers to sex, but it could also be used with reference to a cheese sandwich...one with pickle in...ooh. I've got to the stage in life where food is more exciting than sex. I wonder if some people eat while having sex? Is that a thing? Please send me an email via the author if you know anything about it.

4. The basis of any happy marriage, I find.

Chapter Five

DIE HARD

....

Portslade Cinema has a large picture on the wall above the ticket office, bolted into the wall so no-one can nick it. It's difficult to make out exactly what it is, because the glass has been obscured by dust, smoke and grime. Any decorative function it once possessed has long since been lost. It's still there now; I don't imagine the manager has looked up at it in years, or even noticed it enough to think about changing it. You can just about make out what may be ironwork or scaffolding—it could be Brighton Pier, but it could just as easily be the Eiffel Tower.

However neglected the décor was, the cinema was still an impressive building. It had started out as a Victorian theatre, and boasted an intricately engraved marble pillar entrance and overhanging galleries. The cinema auditorium was adorned with flowing drapes and faded crimson velvet seats. The seats contained little ashtrays, usually full to the brim with decomposing cigarette ends that added a certain *je ne sais quoi* to the musty scent of antique wooden floorboards. In 1982—the year of *E.T.*, *The Thing* and the British nasty *Xtro*—they had had to rip the carpet up on account of an overenthusiastic fungus that was attempting to form a symbiotic relationship with two plastic palm trees either side of the cinema screen.

In 1964, the council had submitted a planning application to knock it down to make way for a car park. A gang of local ladies, led by Molly, had responded by forming a protest group and chaining themselves to the front door, refusing to move until the application had been rescinded. The campaign attracted national news coverage when Molly doubled her efforts by going on hunger strike. Not a single meal passed her lips in nearly three weeks (if it wasn't for the odd sneaky pear drop, she'd have starved to death). The pressure forced the council to reluctantly withdraw their plans, but from then on they refused to fund the maintenance of the building. What remains is a crumbling symbol of female resistance in a world dominated by men obsessed with financial budgets, though they are hopefully more in touch with their feminine sides as a result. The film showing was *Die Hard with a Vengeance*.

Barry and Jo came running in to the ticket office, sweaty and flustered.

'Have I got time for a fag?' asked Jo, already lighting up. Barry shrugged his shoulders. The film had been showing for three weeks, and he'd already seen it twice.

'Shall we sit on the back row?'

'Are you going to try and get off with me then?' Jo grinned, extricating as much nicotine as possible from her rollie.

Barry pretended not to hear and promptly opened the door to the auditorium when she had finished. The place was heaving, and the floorboards creaked beneath them as they navigated their way through the darkness in search of empty seats. Having missed the first twenty minutes of the film, they were thrown into the action as they sat down and started chomping on a bumper box of popcorn. Barry leant over, pointed at the screen, and whispered into Jo's ear.

'If I was in that situation, I'd just turn myself invisible.'

'Really?' Jo raised her eyebrows. 'How about being invisible for a while now and letting me watch the bloody film? I quite like that Bruce Willis; I wouldn't say no.'

Barry grunted, crossed his arms, and slumped into his seat. He managed to sit still for twenty minutes, but couldn't focus on the film. He was completely intoxicated by Jo's presence; the allure of her Spice Girls body spray, her matted eyelashes, fishnet tights, and nicotine breath. He wanted to kiss her, more than he'd ever wanted to do anything.

What if she says no? I couldn't cope with the rejection...not again. OK, get a grip; don't overthink it, just act.

His heart was rattling around his ribcage like a hobnail boot in a tumble dryer. He slowly reached out his arm, then, losing his nerve, quickly pulled it back and scratched his head. Jo was lost in celluloid bliss, transfixed to the screen. Only her right arm moved; a slow, inexorable machine feeding her popcorn. She was blithely unaware of the emotional carnage occurring beside her. Every sinew in Barry's body was tingling, and a bilious sensation erupted in the pit of his stomach. Either it was nerves or he was about to decorate the back of the velvet seat in front of him. Jo moved forward to put her popcorn box on the floor.

This is my chance, it's now or never.

Barry felt like his heart was about to re-enact *Alien* and burst through his chest, but he forced himself sideways, swung his arm around Jo, and gripped her by the waist.

'Shitting heck!' Jo spat out her last mouthful of popcorn grits. 'You almost gave me a heart attack.'

'I'm sorry, I'm sorry.' Barry pulled away quickly and shrank back to the safety of his seat, suddenly wishing he were anywhere other than where he was.

If I never have another date for the rest of my life, it will be too soon.

They pretended to continue watching the film for another ten minutes until Jo finally leant over.

'So are we gonna snog then, or what?'[1]

Barry was dumbstruck, bewildered, and blindsided as she gave him a tender kiss on the lips, winding her arms around him as she did so. They were instantly soaring in a wild embrace, a twilight zone where only they existed. In the background, Mr Willis was raising sweet Armageddon, but all Barry could do was stare drunkenly into Jo's eyes, if they were her eyes—with it being so dark and in such close quarters, all he could really make out was a blurry glimmer. What a kiss it was! Barry had experienced nothing like it; a burning rapture of silky tongues entwining like ivy, electricity firing through all the wires of his body. The world could have ended right then, and he would not have noticed. Even the sugary reek of the snacks and fags of yesteryear[2] had become the scent of heaven to him. It took Jo's overriding need for a nicotine top-up of to temporarily break the spell, and Barry took the chance to nip off for a wee. He soon returned, crossing his legs awkwardly as he sat down.

'The toilets are locked! I'm gonna wet myself!'

'I have that effect on all the boys.'

At that moment, the film stopped. The screen went black, and the auditorium dropped into darkness. Screams could be heard coming from the foyer; and Jo reached out and grabbed Barry's arm. The doors to the screen burst open, and three large figures dressed like samurai warriors stood silhouetted in the doorway. They must have been at least seven feet tall, holding long curved swords that reflected light into the confused faces staring up at them. The largest of them stood in the middle, bull horns protruding out of his steel helmet.

That must be who chased me through the woods!

The second warrior was clad in gold-plated body armour, and the third gripped two razor-sharp *tantō* knives, famously used by the samurai in feudal Japan to slash their victims. The leader signalled to his comrades to block the exits on the opposite side of the auditorium. Barry couldn't make out their faces, but he knew this was no prank. He grabbed Jo's hand and pulled her towards the back of the auditorium, where it was darkest. The three figures stormed the room, scything their weapons into the sea of trapped bodies. The walls of the auditorium echoed with wails of torment and horror as the crowd surged *en masse* toward the rear exit. Despite their efforts, Barry and Jo were caught up in the grid-lock of bodies jammed in the centre of the auditorium. Nobody was able to move as the warriors continued ruth-lessly slicing into the helpless victims before them.

After a few minutes of relentless bloodshed, there were only a handful of people separating them from the approaching warriors. Barry had to come up with a plan, and fast. He looked upwards to the galleries above and noticed the drapes on either side. If they could get to the drapes, they could possibly pull themselves to safety. Barry wriggled and climbed up onto the mass of writhing bodies, proceeding to crowd-surf over to the side of the auditorium. Grabbing two handfuls of drape, he launched himself from the wall and ran back over to Jo, using people's heads as stepping-stones. He reached down and, pulling with all his might, managed to extricate her from the crowd just as the woman in front of her was decapitated by the horned barbarian.

'We've got to climb up to the gallery!' yelled Barry over the din, 'it's the only way out of here.'

Jo grabbed the drape and slowly hauled herself upwards. They were about halfway up when those beneath them, seeing their plan, began pulling themselves up in a frenzy of desperation.

'The drapes won't hold us all!' shouted Jo, hearing a tearing sound coming from the ceiling above them.

Barry managed to pull his ample posterior over the edge of the gallery and quickly stretched his arm down for Jo's hand to lift her up.

'Hurry up, Jo, we've not got much time.'

'I'm not strong enough, Barry, I can't hold—'

The drapes tore from their fixings, sending Jo and countless others hurtling down to the floor below.

Standing on the balcony, Barry stared helplessly into the darkness. The screams had given way to softer groans, but tiny sparks of light still danced on the samurais' blades, giving clues to the circus of horrors still unfolding. Running down the stairs, Barry found a group of female ushers piled in the foyer like a haystack, dead. He picked up an advertising board and ripped off the pole to use as a weapon.

There was an eerie silence in the auditorium. Dismembered bodies littered the aisles, and looking over to the rear exit, he could see the doors were now wide open. Outside on the pavement lay a handful of bloodied survivors. Barry scanned their shell-shocked faces in the desperate hope one of them might be Jo. He couldn't see her, but did recognise an older man from the allotments.

'Charlie! What the hell happened?'

'They looked like something out of a medieval kung fu film…they just…went…mad.' Tears were gushing from the man's vermilion eyes.

'Have you seen a woman with a tattoo on her shoulder?'

'I'm not sure. They went off towards the seafront carrying a blond-haired woman, she was going ballistic.'

Barry took out his pager and quickly typed a message to the doctor:

· · ·

Call police, send to cinema, there's been a massacre.

Running as fast as he could down Portslade High Street, Barry looked up every side alley and in every shop window, but found nothing. Eventually, he reached the seafront and leant breathlessly on the frosty iron promenade railings. Petrol-stained clouds hurried across a blood-black sky, and the salty spray stung his eyes as giant waves crashed against the concrete groynes. Wiping his face, Barry noticed something glimmering on the shingle-scattered tarmac in front of him. Bending down, he realised it was Jo's shiny PVC handbag. The five packs of contraband baccy inside confirmed it. Looking closer, he made out a severed hand lying in the top of the bag. *Please no!* The discovery shot a hot charge of adrenalin through him. Gripping the bag as hard as he could, he sprang to his feet and sprinted along the promenade. Mile upon mile against a bitter salty wind he ran, looking wildly from one side to the other. His boots cut into his heels, but he didn't stop until he reached Brighton. Jo was nowhere to be seen.[3]

---

1. Snog – To kiss passionately using the classic French method. I don't think it's possible to snog without tongues unless you have had yours cut out for lying to the Queen (which still happens in Britain). I'm not sure why it's referred to as a 'French kiss'; surely people were sticking their tongues into each other's mouths before national boundaries were established? It's important to be aware that Scottish people don't do French kissing because of their vulnerability towards fungal infections. Instead, they perform a ritual involving kilts and deep-fried chocolate bars, which is equally enjoyable but less hygienic. I holiday in Scotland every year to do it as often as I can.

   The Scottish attitude towards the English can be a bit confusing at times; .i quite antagonistic, but mixed with great kindness, often taking the form of a back-handed compliment you don't appreciate until later. Take, for example, an incident in Glasgow in 1990, when a young man kindly removed all my teeth for me when I asked him for directions.

This wasn't pleasant at the time, but has since saved me years of expensive dental treatment.

2. A fag in Brit speak is a cigarette. Really. Just a cigarette. Nothing else.

3. Tomorrow may well be bringing better weather, but what consolation would that be for the victims at the cinema tonight? And for the survivors, how could they even begin to explain what they had witnessed? Where was Jo? Was it her they were after? Fucking samurai? Really? So many questions, so little time...

Chapter Six

A HELPING HAND

T he howl from the kitchen window was so loud that it turned on one of the overhead hairdryers downstairs. Molly had awoken to find a severed hand in a PVC handbag on her kitchen table. She tore into the front room and shook Barry awake.

'Why is there a fucking hand in a fucking handbag on my fucking kitchen table?'

Barry wiped his bloodshot eyes. 'Sorry Mum, it's Jo's handbag...there was a situation last night—'

'What kind of situation?'

Barry sat up, flinching as the sheet peeled away from the blisters on his feet.

'These three lunatics came running into the cinema. Nearly everyone was killed, and they kidnapped Jo, I looked everywhere for her. We need to call the police to see if she's been found.'

'Just wait, I'm calling Ril first.' Molly disappeared into the hallway.

Struggling to his feet, Barry turned on the radio in the kitchen, and set about wrapping the hand in cling film. He had feared it belonged to Jo; thankfully, the light of day had painted another picture. Its calloused skin revealed it came from to a much older person and the only way to get Molly off his back would be to bury it in the garden. Covered in soil, Barry was putting his spade back into the shed when a distraught Merril appeared at the garden gate.

'Why didn't you save her? I thought you were a ninja, what the fuck happened?'

'I tried, Ril.' A desperate tiredness made his words breathless and hoarse. 'They had swords, they were cutting everybody to bits. We couldn't move, there were too many people.'

'You crapped yourself, didn't you?'[1]

Barry's voice strengthened with indignation. 'They were seven feet tall with two-metre swords! They were slicing through three people at once.'

'Never mind that,' Merril grabbed Barry by the collar. 'What are you gonna do to get my niece back, you chicken shit?'

Molly came out of the back door and put her arms round Merril.

'Calm down, darling. Let's put the kettle on and talk this through.'

They trundled upstairs and entered the kitchen to hear a newsflash on the radio.

'Police are describing last night's attack on film-goers and staff at Portslade Cinema as unprovoked, remorseless, and apparently motiveless. Unconfirmed reports currently put the number of those killed or injured at 320. Eye-witness accounts are coming in, confirming that three men dressed as samurai warriors and armed with swords and daggers carried out the attack. No guns were used, and one survivor said the ordeal felt like being on a medieval battle-

ground. Police will be making a formal statement at 9 a.m. this morning.'

The pressure was all too much for Barry, and he sat down and collapsed in tears on the kitchen table. 'I tried my hardest to save her, Ril, I really did. Everyone I come into contact with goes missing, first Mindy, then Dad, and now Jo. I think we should go to the police.'

'No police,' said Merril, 'I don't trust them; we're going to do this the Portslade way. We'll turn over every stone, leaf and body part until we flush these fuckers out. I'll get Robbie to put the word around at the hairdressers. It's just a matter of time.'

'These guys were dressed like old fashioned samurai warriors, it was really weird,' said Barry, his head in his hands.

'If this is the way people get their kicks,' said Molly, 'everything's gone to hell.'

Merril slumped down next to Barry and began frantically digging around in Jo's handbag.

'Fuck! Jo's medication is in here, if she misses it for more than 72 hours she could have another seizure...the last one nearly killed her.' Merril grabbed Barry by the arm. 'Do you hear what I'm saying?'

Barry looked at her, wide eyed and ashen-faced. 'It's down to us to save Jo...and we've only got three days.'

---

1. In fairness to Barry, my calculations show he actually over performed by 423%

Chapter Seven

GOLDEN DELICIOUS

Day 1 – 8 a.m.

L ike any other profession, gardening has its good and bad days. A sunny July afternoon spent pruning roses whilst being caressed by a gentle sea breeze constitutes a day of wonder, but perfecting every blade of grass on a bowls green during a frosty spring morning as the rain lashes down and a bitter wind freezes your very soul is not so pleasant.

Barry was tolerant of the formidable conditions a gardener in England is subject to the majority of the time. There was something, however, about the fussy, anally-retentive culture of bowls that pressed his buttons. This added to his increasing feeling that his clients did not understand or fully appreciate his talents. One of the obvious discrepancies between how they saw him and how he saw himself was that Barry didn't see himself as a gardener, but more as an international martial arts superstar.[1]

Mrs Caswell of The Portslade Premier Bowls Academy had left detailed instructions pinned to the door of the tool shed about how today's job should proceed. Each task had a little box that she expected to be ticked before commencing with the next job. An additional list was pinned next to the first, stating all the machinery, tools and products required. Below this list was a further list explaining handling and maintenance procedures for the aforementioned gadgetry. Barry put his glasses on, glanced over the carefully constructed paperwork, and chuckled to himself. There was more chance of Attila the Hun winning a posthumous Nobel Peace Prize than there was of him following those instructions. He would do what he always did; make a couple of runs with the power mower and aerator, then mix up 30 gallons of fertiliser and herbicide and slap it on top of the green like a varnish. Bish bash bosh,[2] job done.

The day didn't look to be getting off to the best of starts. The aeration machine had broken down, so Barry was forced to borrow an antiquated manual aerator from Brian. It was essentially a large rolling drum with huge spikes jutting out of it that poked holes in the turf as you pushed it along; the sort of contraption that would look more at home in a museum of medieval war than in a garden shed. Barry slipped into his work overalls and wheeled the aerator onto the green.

He was just about to get started when a hideous stench invaded his nostrils. It was hard to place the smell exactly; somewhere in the region of septic tank and rotting fish carcass. Barry scoured the barrel of the aerator for fear that a small mammal may have been skewered there, but there was nothing. He searched every inch of the bowling green, but couldn't discover where the smell was coming from—until he put his hand into his coat pocket and found the discarded remains of Molly's toxic gourmet casserole. The orange gunge had mutated, and appeared to be crawling up his hand. Barry dropped to the ground, wiped his hands on the grass, then quickly emptied the contents of his pocket onto the green.

Close call, thought Barry, vowing never to set foot in the kitchen when Molly was cooking ever again. Apart from when it was fish fingers, of course.

Barry grabbed the large iron bar of the aerator and set to work running it up and down the green in parallel lines.[3] The rain was pouring down faster and faster—it was a howling sea gale that had blown in from the North Atlantic Ocean, coming in at such an angle as to hit Barry directly in the eyes. There is a saying in gardening: 'there is no such thing as bad weather, only bad clothing.' Whoever came out with that obviously hadn't been out in this kind of a hell-storm. Call him a glutton for punishment, but Barry pushed on regardless, the aerator barrel before his feet making little holes that promptly filled with water. To add to his suffering, Mrs Caswell's pernicious vocal tones played and replayed in his head like a novelty singing fish with failing batteries. '*We need to prevent the green from becoming too compacted…I'm warning you, Mr Harris.*'

. . .

With gritted teeth and the tenacity of a mountain goat, Barry eventually made it to his final pass of the green. He reached the sacred middle runway, which was always best left until last. It had to be treated with the utmost caution given that it was the one bit of the green that was actually used for the game itself. The rain was still lashing down, so Barry put on a baseball cap to try and maintain his line of vision. He moved carefully forward, slowly pushing the contraption in front of him. The water had now penetrated his boots, and every footstep caused a slurping sound as he pounded forward. The end was in sight as Barry approached the area the bowler places the mat on and makes his play from. He was about to congratulate himself when he slipped on Molly's casserole, the aerator flew out of his hands, and he landed face-first into the soggy grass. Looking up, he witnessed the aerator happily tearing up the remainder of the sacred middle runway.

'Shit, shit, shit!' shouted Barry as he jumped to his feet and gawked at the muddy hole that now graced the bowls lawn. He paced up and down the green, staring at the devastation he had created. The most mature and professional course of action would be to take responsibility for his mistake by paying to have the green re-turfed and apologising profusely to the board of directors. Barry understood this. After only a few minutes of reflection, however, he decided instead to bundle the aerator into the back of his van and split, hoping no one had clocked him.[4] When Mrs Caswell tracked him down, he would naturally deny all knowledge of the incident. It was an utterly foolproof plan. Barry ended up back on Portslade High Street in the welcoming embrace of the Steaming Hotties I with a gut-busting fry-up in front of him.

Civilisation at last.

. . .

Pushing his plate away, he noticed it had stopped raining. Having a vague suspicion he may not be getting paid for his morning's work, Barry thought he would move on to the far less vexing task of pruning Mrs Hill's Golden Delicious apple tree.[5] Mrs Hill was a dear old friend of Molly's from the hairdressers and was always pleased to see Barry.

'Now, I've left you a flask of coffee by the back door. Doctor Harper is popping round soon, my veins have been giving me jip; will you be OK without me for an hour or so?'[6]

'That's fine, I'll be busy up your tree most of the time anyway,' replied Barry. Herein lay a particular conundrum, however. Whilst Barry was happy being left alone, it did come with its own set of problems. A perennially awkward aspect of being a gardener is toilet access as customers are often out at work, and town gardens are usually overlooked, making it tricky to relieve yourself in the bushes without causing offence. Two of the best things you can hope for when taking on a job were that there was an unlocked shed and/or a watering can at your disposal. Mrs Hill's garden had neither, so what was a boy to do? Luckily, Barry had been in this situation many times before, and had already engaged in a bit of lateral thinking. After many long nights experimenting with designs and formulas, only to reject them due to system blockages or faulty connecting valves, all the elements had fallen into place when Barry had a eureka moment that would revolutionise his life. He invented a strap-on catheter using an old plastic milk bottle and a length of hosepipe just wide enough for comfort[7], and had meticulously secured the constituent parts of his invention together. First, he glued the hosepipe to the bottle, which was strapped to his outer right thigh using elastic repurposed from Molly's favourite support bra. The pipe was then taped, ever so carefully, to his you-know-what. Naturally the product would have to go through a beta-testing phase—he was wearing it for the first time this afternoon—but should it be successful, Barry was seriously considering marketing it to other gardeners.

Clambering onto an old wooden ladder that Mrs Hill had put out for him, Barry's foot went clean through the first rung, exposing a colony of ferocious woodworm that had long since divested it of any structural integrity. Unperturbed, Barry shimmied up into the dense branches of the apple tree, took out his pruning saw, and surveyed the mass of gnarled branches surrounding him. One of the few things that Barry remembered from horticultural college was the tree pruning mantra of 'The Three "D"s'. When deciding what to saw off, you should always remove the dead, diseased and damaged branches first. Knowing this, Barry always felt confident he would do a good job.[8] Balancing precariously, he shepherded a cassette of *Now That's What I Call Music 30* into his portable cassette player and started sawing away at the offending branches.[9]

Lost in sweet disco tunes and covered in wood shavings, Barry became aware of a rumbling in his guts. The next thing he knew, the tree had started to shake, followed by intermittent sharp thuds, *crack, crack, crack*. Barry looked down and saw the largest of the samurai warriors from the cinema hacking into the trunk, his horned hat tangled in the branches as splinters of wood flew into the air. Stony faced, the warrior smashed his sword into the tree with uniform strikes like a clockwork soldier. Barry clambered as high up the tree as he could, though he had already begun sawing into some of the branches, and wasn't confident they would hold his weight. Briefly wondering if this was where he was going to meet his maker, Barry's attention was suddenly grabbed by

Mrs Hill appearing at the bottom of the tree holding a tray with hot chocolate and crumpets.

'I didn't realise you had a friend working with you today, Barry! Would you like some crumpets too?' asked Mrs Hill, smiling at the warrior.

Without hesitation, the samurai walked over to Mrs Hill, raised his sword high in the air, and sliced her evenly in two, a perfect symmetry of hate. If it hadn't been so horrific, you could have almost been impressed with the accuracy.

'No!' screamed Barry as the two halves of Mrs Hill fell away in opposite directions, and blood-splattered crumpets rolled through the grass like funny little discs in a macabre summer game. From his vantage point, Barry watched the samurai drag half of Mrs Hill into the bushes, and it dawned on Barry that he had one, albeit futile, option left: Dr Harper. He ripped the pager out of his pocket and typed:

Emergency, Mrs Hill's back garden, bring weapon.

As the Samurai turned his attention back towards Barry, he decided to change tack and jabbed his sword upwards into the tree. This forced Barry higher up the branches, which started to crack under his weight. Barry decided his only option was to jump over the samurai and try to run for it, but the exertion of his launch split the branch and sent him cascading downwards. He found himself wedged between two lower branches, dangling just above the warrior like a sitting duck. The samurai paused, mopped his brow—Barry wasn't going anywhere—and mumbled something to himself in Japanese.

'Masutā wa shiawase ni naru.'

Barry had only picked up a few morsels of Japanese from

his father, but could make out that this had something to do with 'making the master happy'; whatever that meant. The samurai stepped closer and raised his blade, blood dripping from the shiny steel tip. Just as he was a about to strike, Dr Harper jumped out of the bushes and threw both his arms around the samurai, attempting some kind of weird bear hug.

'Don't worry Barry, I've got him, you make your escape!'

'I can't, I'm stuck.'

The samurai flung the doctor into the bushes, where he landed like a sack of potatoes, and turned back to Barry. Reaching up, he tried to dislodge him from the tree, yanking at his belt to try and drag him down. Dr Harper separated himself from the foliage and got to his feet.

'It's OK, Barry, I've definitely got him this time!' The doctor went for a rugby tackle; he used to be a scrum half back in the day. This knocked the warrior backwards, causing him to pull Barry's belt so hard it snapped, sending his trousers to his ankles. The samurai grabbed Dr Harper and slammed him against the tree, wrapping his crane-like hands around the doctor's neck. He screamed, *'Anata wa ima shinu!'* into the doctor's face, tightening his grip.

Barry had a hunch this had something to do with the promise of death being fairly imminent. The doctor's arms flailed as the colour quickly drained from his face, reaching out desperately for anything he could use to beat his attacker off with. He grabbed upward, finding Barry's leg and the tubing strapped to it.

'Doctor, careful with that, it's—'

The doctor yanked at the hosepipe, pulling it away from the milk bottle reservoir and causing the warm liquid contents to flood down into the open mouth of the samurai.

'Ahheee!' howled the warrior, furiously spitting the contents over the doctor and momentarily loosening his grip.

'Urgh!' groaned the doctor, who had just availed himself of the opportunity to take a deep breath in.

'Sorry, that was my piss pot,' said Barry.

The warrior, now apoplectic, appeared to have taken the incident rather personally. He ripped the iron body armour from his chest and grabbed two of the tree's main branches, shaking them with a rage of titanic proportions. Deep moans rose out of the heart of the tree until, finally, it could take no more, and snapped, crashing down on top of its three agitators. Amongst the blood, sawdust, and broken bodies, there was a momentary stillness before the rain started to lash down again.[10]

---

1. One of many nagging sources of dissonance within Barry's mental landscape. Bless him.
2. 'Bish bash bosh' is a way of saying something is simple if carried out in a certain way. Normally used when there are three steps to a process.
3. The theory behind this practice is that it prevents soil compaction and brings much needed oxygen to the roots of the grass. The fact that they are then saturated in petroleum-derived synthetic chemicals always seems a bit odd to my mind. I hope you realise I am trying to educate you as well as entertain you? All for free. I'm like a modern-day wandering saint serving humanity, except more sophisticated.
4. If someone's 'clocked' you, it means they have seen you.
5. I could have gone for the 'Barry was going to trim Mrs Hill's Bush' gag here. However, not only is it obvious, but it also belongs to the narrative of the phallocentric agenda, and I'm aiming higher here. Not only am I educating you and making you laugh, I am also transcending dominant paradigms of unconscious prejudice. I'd like you to see me as the Che Guevara of saucy pulp fiction. See what I mean about being sophisticated?
6. Jip (or Gyp) – means pain or trouble.
7. Who says gardeners (who are also ninjas) can't be maverick inventors too? Had Barry been born a hundred years earlier, there is no doubt Thomas Edison would have witnessed his brilliance and gone back to selling sweets at railway stations. I've invented some pretty cool stuff myself. One is a remote-view app for a camera that clings to a person's face and disguises itself as a freckle while filming everything they do. I use one on Barry. Cool, huh? I might show you more later, if you behave.
8. The fact that you should only prune apple trees in winter was one of the things he'd obviously forgotten.

9. If the government ever offer apprenticeship schemes for 'Gardening Inventor Disco Ninjas' (which might be possible post-Brexit), Barry could write the curriculum.

10. I caught the whole show from the bushes. It was damn shame about dear old Mrs Hill. Those crumpets were delicious though, every cloud. Between me and you, I can't see how Barry can defeat this enemy. I'll probably have to step in and help him myself soon. Then the sparks will start flying, just you wait.

Chapter Eight

JEFFREY AND THE PLEASURE FACTORY

Day 1 – 11 a.m.

Hidden away down the backstreets of Portslade lies an abandoned industrial estate once home to a thriving community of fish factories that provided abundant employment to the local people. Unfortunately, those days are gone. The fishermen blamed the 1983 European fishing quotas for driving them out of existence. European policy makers, however, believed it was a necessary move to ensure fish supplies over the coming decades. Whatever the truth of the matter, all that remains of those times is the drunken nostalgia in the Goat and Ferret Pub, the local history pamphlets, and the fading conversations of the elderly population. Now the estate is a smorgasbord of discarded fridges, empty beer cans, and broken windows. Silent but for the flapping of shredded plastic bags caught in the buddleja growing through the cracks in the tarmac, and deserted except for the sparrow colonies that have taken up residence in the factory rooves, the occasional gang of pot-smoking teenagers, and one solitary business: The Pleasure Factory.

This was also the place the charming samurai gentlemen brought Jo the night they abducted her. Having just introduced her face to a brick wall, one of the warriors kindly explained to her in broken English that they had been watching her for months. Why they had been doing this was not clear, however. They had then locked her into a cramped, dimly lit storeroom without food or water, and her repeated requests for medicine had fallen on deaf ears.

The storeroom contained boxes upon boxes of every possible erotic love aid known to human existence, and clothing rails provided costumes for all those inclined towards a bit of naughty cosplay. Be it Chewbacca or Barbie, one could safely re-enact their dressing up kinks with no questions asked.[1] When Jo's boss Jeffrey arrived for work the following morning, they made him stand at the front door and send the rest of the arriving staff back home. As the place was a not-quite-legal enterprise, no one batted an eyelid when this kind of thing happened. Anyway, it was a great opportunity to go home and watch *Neighbours*.

Unfortunately, Jeffrey was not allowed to leave, and after being kindly provided with a knuckle sandwich, was locked up with Jo. Appearances are often deceptive, but Jeffrey seemed to be the man least likely to be running a sex business. He was only forty-two, but liked nothing better than to stay in and play dominoes of an evening. His other hobbies included reading about dominoes and building model aeroplanes. Whenever any of his staff invited him on a night out, he refused, as going to bed later than 9 p.m. was strictly off the menu. The Pleasure Factory had been started by his late wife Valerie, who firmly believed British people needed to have more sex if the Empire was to ever find its feet again. Jeffrey had sworn on her deathbed that, as long as he lived, he would never sell the business.

'Jo, wake up...wake up, for heaven's sake.' Jeffrey shook Jo's shoulder.

Jo was conscious, but had so little energy she could barely move. She tried opening her eyes, but her eyelids felt like fine grade sandpaper and the sun coming through a small window almost burnt her skin. The pain in her head was insane, like termites were slowly devouring her brain. Up above them on the first floor, the samurai could be heard chanting some kind of incantation, repeating the name 'Sambō-Kōjin' over and over in an eerie drone.

Jo finally managed to open her eyes, and with Jeffrey's assistance, she got to her feet, but soon slumped against the wall, the room turning like a kaleidoscope. Jeffrey took his jacket off and wrapped it around her, then picked up a mug containing cold coffee dregs and raised it to her mouth, 'Drink this, it's better than nothing.'

However scared Jo was, she wouldn't admit it, not even to herself. Life had forced her to be tough for so long it was second nature.[2]

'Who the hell are they?'

Jo stared back at Jeffrey, mute.

'With the costumes, I thought they might be disgruntled customers.'

Shaking her head, Jo spoke softly, 'I think they are the real McCoy.'

'Real samurai? In Portslade, in 1995? How?[3]' Jeffrey pulled his glasses down and stared at Jo over the rims.

'A better question would be, how the hell are we going to get out?'

Jo looked up at a small window about three meters up the wall.

'Do you think we could make it?

Jo shook her head. 'I'm not feeling strong enough.'

Jeffery rushed over to the desk and rifled through its drawers. 'I know they are in here...' He turned around, holding a set of keys. 'We can get out of this door at least.'

'Into the showroom? Far too risky...I've seen what they do to people.'

'What choice do we have?' said Jeffrey, wiping the sweat from his forehead with his shirt sleeve. 'What will happen if you don't get your medication?'

'We both know the answer to that.'

Upstairs, the incantation grew louder: 'Sambō-Kōjin, Sambō-Kōjin...'

'I've got an idea,' said Jo, pointing to the clothing rail. 'Put on that latex bodysuit.'

'Why would I do that?'

'You can hide in the bondage section if you hear them coming.'

Jeffery walked over to the clothing rail, tutting to himself.

'You got a better plan?'

Stepping reluctantly into a suit, Jeffrey breathed in deeply and zipped himself up as far as he could before turning to let Jo finish the job.

'You might even freak them out a bit!' said Jo.

Above them, the samurai began pounding the hilts of their swords on the floor as the ceremony rose to a fever pitch.

'Quick,' said Jo, 'while they're occupied. Go get help!'

Jeffrey crept across the room, turned the key in the lock, and ever-so-carefully pulled the cool steel door towards him. The hallway was a dark abyss, beckoning him forwards. Turning back to Jo, Jeffrey took hold of her arms. 'I'll be back before you—'

The next thing Jo saw was a sword emerging from Jeffery's

chest. Without a sound, he fell to his knees, his eyes still open as if unaware he was now a dead man. The unmistakable horned hat of the lead samurai rose up from behind Jeffery's lifeless body.

'This is what happen to you next time.'

'What have I ever done to you?'

In answer, the samurai wrenched his sword from Jeffrey's body and pushed him to the ground.

Jo picked up the coffee cup and sent it careering towards the warrior, it bounced off his chest, and he hardly noticed. 'I need my medication, you bastard!'

'Why? You dead soon anyway.' The nameless warrior took the key from the lock and slammed the door behind him.

Jo's vision was a blur, her fury the only thing keeping her upright. She had to get some kind of message to the outside world. The only idea her addled brain came up with horrified her, but she had no choice. Kneeling down beside Jeffrey, she whispered into his ear, 'Forgive me.'

She sunk her fingers into his wound and scooped up globules of fresh blood, which she smeared over the top of a broom handle. She then reached up and painted the word '*HELP*' in big letters across the window above her. No sooner had she finished than the room spun like a Ferris wheel. She tried to steady herself, but her legs gave way, and she fell face first into Jeffery's bloody chest.

---

1. That is until your wife catches you sitting on the sofa dressed as a Teletubby, eating chocolate with her underwear on your head. Never again.
2. Why does bad shit happen to good people? I'll never work that one out. Jo was the kindest soul you could ever meet, but always seemed to get such a rough ride. I used to share a house with one of her exes, and he treated her miserably. It got so bad I was forced to teach him a lesson. I put him through a meat grinder and turned him into a Shepherd's Pie. The trick is not to use much black pepper; he's sitting in my deep freeze now with a much more agreeable attitude.

3. How indeed! The last time I witnessed time-reversal symmetry to this degree was...never. Forget everything you think you know about quantum non-invasive measurements, and trust me when I tell you that my calculations have shown it would easier to swim to Mars than for this event to have occurred. I told you this journey wouldn't be easy, didn't I? Still think you can hack it?

Chapter Nine

LEGS AIKIDO

Day 1 – 5 p.m.

Barry woke to the sight of Dr Harper's beard, which wafted of pipe smoke and stale urine. Having a tendency towards pognophobia,[1] Barry was unsure what disgusted him the most, the hairiness or the stink.

The collapsed apple tree had forced Barry and the doctor into a rather compromising position; one that could be construed as less than innocent, seeing as they were pinned firmly into the missionary position. This wouldn't have been much of a problem in and of itself, but they also had a seven-foot samurai warrior lying on top of them. Thankfully, he was completely sparko.

Barry whispered into the doctor's beard.

'Doctor.'

'Hmm...?' replied the doctor, twitching his nose.

'Shhh...wake up, but quietly.'

'Wha-what?'

'Shut your cake hole.'[2] Barry whispered as urgently as he dared.

The doctor's eyes sprang open as he took in the samurai. 'Good heavens, we're in a bit of a predicament.'

'You...could...say that,' replied Barry, struggling to breathe.

After wriggling, the doctor managed to free one of his arms. 'I may be able to get myself out, but only if you can hoist our friend up a bit.'

'Sure, no problem,' heaved Barry, rolling his bulging eyes.

'One...two...and *lift*.'

Barry pushed upwards with all his effort as the doctor grabbed the base of the fractured tree trunk and started to pull himself loose. Barry was turning an interesting shade of periwinkle under the immense weight of a nemesis who, much to his horror, began murmuring.

'Uhhuh?'

'Hurry up!' Barry huffed, 'he's coming round.'

The doctor gave himself one more almighty tug and managed to get clear of his entanglement, sending Barry and the samurai crashing to the ground.

'Aieeee!' screamed the samurai, who had woken up in an even shittier mood than he had been in earlier.

'Pull me out,' begged Barry, 'he's gonna kill me!'

Lying face-first on Barry's back, pinned down by the tree and burdened by his armour, the samurai was unable to move; his only means of attack was his mouth.

'Ah! He's just taken a bite out of my ear. Do something.'

The doctor ran around Mrs Hill's garden, desperately searching for any kind of weapon to use.

'Barry, I can't find anything!' With that, the doctor tripped over the half of Mrs Hill still lying in the grass. Looking closer, he realised that one of her legs had come away from the rest her body. Without a second thought, he scooped it up and bashed the samurai over the head with it.

'That's making it worse!' shouted Barry. 'He's started on my other ear! Stick her foot in his mouth.'

'What?'

'Shove it in as far as it goes!'

Being smeared with oozing blood, it was frustratingly difficult for the doctor to get a decent purchase on Mrs Hill's foot in order to straighten it enough for insertion. He had to resort to banging the leg on top of the samurai's head a few more times before ramming it with all his strength into the warrior's gnashing jaws. The samurai's bulbus eyes were as wide as an owl's as he gagged on dear old Mrs Hill's leg, giving Barry the opportunity he needed to scramble out from under him. Clambering to his feet, he joined the doctor's efforts to wedge the leg ever further into the gullet of the raging samurai.

'Let's try and get it in up to her knee,' said Barry.

However, with the added freedom of more space beneath him, the samurai managed to free his arms enough to begin snapping the branches of his wooden prison.

'I think it's time to leave now, Barry, this volcano is about to erupt.'

Giving one last thrust of Mrs Hill's leg, Barry and the doctor sprinted out of the garden and onto the High Street. Briskly losing themselves in the crowds of people at the weekly market, they ducked into the sanctuary of Portslade Library. The bay window of the secluded archives section on the first floor gave them the perfect vantage point from which to view the street below. As anyone who has ever witnessed a psychopathic seven-foot samurai running down the road with half a leg hanging out of his mouth will know, it is rather entertaining. Watching the samurai fly past them, the duo realised they were in the clear, at least for now.

As the pair were leaving the library, they walked past the science section. Barry was certain he saw Keith, the Basset Hound from his neighbour's garden, with his head buried in a book on astrophysics.

'Doctor, did you just see...?'

'What's that?'

'Oh nothing, I think I need to lie down.'[3]

Barry arrived home sweaty, starving, and still fishing bits of Dr Harper's beard from between his teeth. Molly came running in from the kitchen to see her blood-splattered son sitting on the futon.

'What's happened to your ears?'

'I had a bit of a run-in with one of those samurais.'

Molly gave him to the strongest hug she could muster, then disappeared into the bathroom, returning with antiseptic cream and plasters.

'I can't lose you as well as Jo and...' Molly trailed off, her bottom lip wobbling as she dabbed at Barry's ears.

'Ouch...You won't, Mum.' Barry knew what was coming next.

'I'm scared they're never coming back.' Tears trickled down Molly's face now. Exhausted and in no small amount of shock, Barry couldn't stop himself from joining her. Together they sat, weeping uncontrollably.

'I...miss them...too, Mum.' Barry tried to get a grip on himself. 'I trust Dad; he'll find a way back to us, but we need to find Jo first.'

Molly blew her nose and looked at Barry through tear-misted eyes. 'I know, love, I know.'

'I'll make us some hot chocolate.' Barry headed for the kitchen, wiping his face with his beanie.

When he returned with two steaming mugs, Molly carefully applied plasters to his chewed-up ears, then put on her favourite Motörhead album, for what problems in life can't be cured by the simple act of listening to Motörhead?

The doorbell rang. Predictably, Merril appeared in the doorway five minutes later, sweating like a sumo.

'There's no information on where we can find these buggers anywhere. I've exhausted all my contacts—'

'No one knows nuffin'?' said Molly. 'In the whole of Portslade?'

'Not a dicky bird. It's like they're ghosts.' Merril was trembling as she sat down. She rooted in her handbag for her tobacco pouch.

'Mol, I'm shit scared. There was this radio program about diabetic seizures last night...' Merril paused to make a cigarette, but tore the rolling paper and sent tobacco all over her lap.

'Come here, darling.' Molly went over and put her arms around her, and Merril wept silently into her shoulder. 'That's it, you get it out girl.'

Barry rolled a cigarette and handed it to Merril.

'Thanks, love.' Merril wiped her nose with the back of her hand and placed the pencil-thin rollie between her teeth. 'I need this.' A long string of snot stretched from her nose to the end of the cigarette as she lit up and inhaled hard. She stared intently at Molly and Barry.

'The time has come, boys and girls.'

'You don't mean—?' Molly clutched at Merril's arm.

'I do.'

'Are you sure it's safe?'

'No,' Merril sucked even harder, smearing sickly vermilion lipstick on her rollie and attempting a battle-weary stare of fateful indifference. 'But do you know what my grandad told me his best mate Charlie said just before they went over the top in 1916? "We may be staring into the abyss, but we still have our eyes."'

Barry pushed out his bottom lip and scratched a tuft of hair on the top of his head in an unintentional impression of Stan Laurel. 'So...what does that mean?'

'I ain't got a fucking clue, but my grandad survived and Charlie stepped on a land mine.'

Barry scratched his tuft some more.

'Makes you fink, don't it?' said Molly, shaking her head philosophically and trying out Merril's faraway look.

'Alright if I stay here tonight, Mol? Tomorrow, we're all gonna have a lovely day out.'

'Where are we going?' asked Barry.

'To see a lunatic about three psychopaths.'

---

1. Pogonophobia is the fear of people with beards. It's a real thing. I grew a massive beard once, and my wife made me sleep in the shed. I had to wax before being allowed back in the house. It wasn't easy, as I'm what you might call hirsute, or a furry love machine.

2. Cakehole – Mouth. Probably called that because it's where we put our cake. Not me though, If I eat too much I get high cholesterol and have to use special margarine.

3. And what should be so strange about a dog that understands science, or any animal for that matter? You humans are so anthropocentric. You really should really try and get out of this galaxy every now and then.

Chapter Ten

THE ORACLE OF PORTSLADE

Day 2 – 9 a.m.

There are times in life when—out of desperation—a person is forced to contemplate actions they wouldn't ordinarily consider. During these times, they may need to press 'pause' on their moral code until normal conditions resume. A trip to see the Oracle of Portslade constitutes one such occasion. Everybody has heard about the Oracle, though if ever there were someone—or something—cloaked in mystery, it is him. Some believe he is the beating pulse of Portslade's criminal underworld; a violent deranged lunatic who uses his enemies as shark bait while he runs the legitimate face of his enterprise, Bertie's Tackle; a fishing supplies shop on the edge of darkest Portslade. Others believe he is a spiritual master whose celestial powers make him not quite human, and if you put yourself at his mercy, he will cure your every affliction. Whether his knowledge and power come from transcendental wisdom, the realm of the spirits, or the fact that most people owe him a favour, the truth is that when you are fresh out of luck in Portslade, it is time for you to make the pilgrimage and kneel before the Oracle.

Barry, Molly and Merril set off on their intrepid journey. They took the route along the seafront by the fish market. Squeezing round the vats of bubbling tarmac being applied to the new road surface, they hurried past an old skip, from which a burning mattress was spewing a black toxic fog. They took a shortcut by ducking into the affectionately-named 'Dog Shit Alley' which brought them out by the bins at the back of Debenhams where the town's homeless contingent lived, and travelled a mere hundred metres past the power station before they reached their destination. Barry had wanted to take the bus, but Molly insisted the fresh air would do them all good.

Standing at the closed door of Bertie's Tackle and contemplating the worn, chipped bars across the doors that made it look more like a lock-up than a retail establishment, Molly held her handbag firmly against her belly in a bid to stop herself from shaking so much.

'You have to knock three times, wait exactly a minute, then knock again,' said Merril, edging Molly forward.

Molly raised her quivering hand and struck the metal knocker against the door. *Clack, clack, clack.* Her eyes darted between her wristwatch, Barry, and Merril for what seemed like an hour, before she reached for the knocker again...*clack*. The door opened several inches to reveal a pair of eyes in the gloom—rather lower than they expected—before the door was pulled far enough open to allow the light outside to fall upon a man no taller than three feet with a fire-red beard and an Abraham Lincoln top hat.

'.sgniteerG'

'You what, dear?' said Molly, squinting.

'.dias I sgniteerG' repeated the man, gesturing them to follow him as he marched backwards into the fishing shop.

'.yaw siht, yaw sihT'

Bertie led them through the shop, past its rods and nets dangling from the ceiling, and into an even more poorly-lit room at the rear of the building. Above the door was a wooden engraved sign that read, *'The Inner Sanctum'*. Molly spluttered on entering due to the cloud of sandalwood incense hording the air. Chanting could be heard from a tinny speaker, and a row of white candles along the back wall created ghostlike shadows that danced at the feet of the three guests.

The red-bearded, diminutive Abraham Lincoln marched into the fog to be greeted by a deep raspy voice. 'Good boy, Bertie! You are excused.'

As Bertie trudged back to his duties, the swirling incense seemed to take on a human form.

'I've been expecting you,' said the small rotund man in a black silk robe materialising before them.

Molly gasped and grabbed Barry's arm.

Two middle-aged men wearing fishnet stockings and leather army boots also emerged, gently wafting their guru with long-handled fans made from peacock feathers.

The well-padded sage held a small stained tea towel, which he used to mop up the sweat beads escaping from his forehead.[1] 'Please make yourself comfortable.' He pointed to some meditation cushions arranged on a cashmere rug at the base of the bespoke cedar wooden platform that he and his acolytes occupied. Engraved on a plaque set on the front of the platform were the words *'Find yourself through me'*.

'What language was he speaking?' asked Merril, her eyes trying to avoid the fanbearers as she shifted awkwardly on a lumpy cushion.

'Bertie is speaking English, but backwards. In fact, he

does everything backwards. People are addicted to going forwards, because they seem to think they will arrive somewhere. Where do you think that destination might be?' asked the Oracle.

'Happiness?' piped up Molly, looking quite pleased with her answer.

'That comes and goes,' said the Oracle. 'It is not a destination, it is a by-product of something far greater.'

'Meaning?' mumbled Barry, staring at the faded pattern on his cushion and feeling less sure of himself now he had spoken.

'Yes, young man, meaning indeed! Did you know that in all our communication there is conscious, forward linear meaning, and backwards, unconscious, deeper meaning? Bertie is on a journey to find that hidden meaning.'

'What will he do when he finds it?' asked Merril a little testily. Barry winced, afraid that Merril might not make it through the next five minutes.

'No one knows what their karma has in store for them, do they? Take Freckles here.' He pointed to one of his fan-bearers. 'He left university with a PhD in Business Studies and set up his own financial analysis company. He was a billionaire by the age of 26, and a financial guru to every upwardly mobile yuppie in The City. One day, he got home from work to find his hamster had died. The grief devastated him so much he walked out of his mansion, leaving the keys in the door, and started living rough on the streets. I found him living in a dustbin under Brighton Pier, a tin of cat food in one hand and a bottle of meths in the other. He hadn't been near a bar of soap in five years, and had no teeth left. I took him in, bathed him, and rebuilt him into the fine figure of a man you see before you.'

'Why is he wearing stockings?' enquired Molly, balancing precariously on the edge of her cushion.

'It's a sign of respect for all my kindness.' Freckles lost his rhythm for a moment, recovering with a rather elaborate adjustment of his grip on the fan. The Oracle indulged him with a fleeting smirk. '

But enough about us; how about you? It seems you are in a serious predicament, mmm?"

'How do you know? asked Barry, still not daring to look directly up at the Oracle.

'I am the all-seeing eye of Portslade. I know everything... most of the time. Lately, however, there has been a fourth-dimension portal disturbance, the first in Portslade for a thousand years.'

'See, Quincy? I told you that's what it was.' Freckles whispered furiously at the other fan-bearer.

Quincy tutted and threw his head back, matching his adversary's indignant wheeze. 'Oh, piss off, *I* told *you* that!'

The Oracle grinned, revealing wonky, nicotine-stained teeth. 'Ignore them, they do like to bicker.' He then proceeded to mop the sweat from his armpits with the tea towel and wring the moisture into a spittoon placed on his platform.[2]

Merril got up and walked over to grab the Oracle's slimy hand. 'My niece has been kidnapped, and without her medicine she could die at any time. Please help us find her.'

Quincy cast a death-glare at Freckles, seemingly unaffected by Merril's distress. 'There's only one disturbance in my portal...'

'Oh, why don't you fuck off back to your mum's house?' Freckles spat back.

'SHUT UP, BOTH OF YOU!' bellowed The Oracle. 'How many times do I have to tell you, not when we have guests! Now my dear, due to the disturbances, I will need to enter a trance and allow a Tibetan Deity to take possession of my earthly form in order to find the answers you seek. There are dangers involved, and I have my flock to consider. Who would look after Quincy, Freckles, and Bertie Backwards if anything happened to me, mmm?'

'OK, how much?' Merril's hands were firmly rooted on her hips.

'A grand should do it.'

'Let's call it a monkey, shall we?'[3] Having worked in Portslade Market for some thirty years, Merril could sell holy water to Beelzebub.

The Oracle nodded his approval and clashed his hands together like cymbals. Bertie Backwards shuffled into the room, money changed hands, and when Bertie had leafed through the notes and given his master the nod, Freckles loosened the Oracle's robe and Quincy wrapped a white silk scarf around his forehead. Raising his hands in the air as if conducting an orchestra, the Oracle intoned a series of baritone vocal warm-ups, 'Lul lul lul lul laaaa. Hi hi hi hi haaa.' Picking up a piece of old parchment—that may or may not have shown the esoteric words *'The Racing News'* on its outer side, it was hard to see through the incense fog—the Oracle began reciting an incantation:

'Great Warrior Queen!
  I come to you today,
  With fire and incense,
  With passion and hope,
  At a time of great peril,
  Hear my call, o sacred deity,
  Mollie Sugden,
  Guide us with your wisdom,
  Use me as your vessel!'

                              .   .   .

Merril lent over and whispered in Barry's ear, 'Isn't she from—?'

'Shh,' replied Barry, putting a finger to his lips and his other hand on his belly in an attempt to stifle its rumbling. Bertie grabbed hold of his hat and jumped up and down while the fan-bearers furiously ventilated their sweaty guru. The Oracle rocked backwards and forwards and his eyes rolled up into their sockets, leaving only the white sclera gaping at his visitors.

'I am speaking to you from the other side....a grave danger is upon you...you should be very, very scared.'

'Thank you, Mrs Sugden,' said Merril, holding onto to Barry for support. 'What are these monsters that have kidnapped my niece?'

'They are mercenary samurai demons from the ancient shadow worlds. They are evil incarnate. You should be very, very sc—'

'Yeah alright, we got that bit,' said Merril, raising her voice. 'Are you saying they are dead?'

'They are neither alive nor dead.'

'Why did they kidnap Jo?' asked Molly, peeping out from behind Barry.

'To answer this question, you have to think like a samurai. These warriors are highly trained to the peak of physical endurance, guided by strict moral principles of loyalty and honour. No hardship will break their resolve, and no suffering will alter their determination. They will stop at nothing to get what they want, so you must ask, "What is it they are after?" It must be something very, very important to them.'

'Is it because she's got big tits?' asked Merril.

Everyone in the room shook their heads in unison. Barry turned to her and made a zip gesture across his lips. The Oracle was writhing on his platform, perspiring like a yeti on a sun lounger. He opened one of his eyes, looked around, then closed it again as he came to sudden halt.

'The answer lies much deeper. It may have something to do with Barry's father Yamoshi's disappearance. You must go to the amphitheatre[4] at noon on the day of the full moon. That is where you will find them. My last message is this: the only thing that can save you is staring you directly in the face.' The Oracle held up his hand to indicate that the deity had now left his mortal flesh, and Bertie came bounding over backwards to help the Oracle off the platform and out of the room.

'.retsam yaw sihT'

'The Oracle needs to rest now,' said Freckles. 'I'll show you all out.'

Back in the hustle and bustle of the High Street, squinting from the sunshine, they still weren't exactly sure what had happened. They sat down on a bench outside a chip shop and collected themselves.

'He seemed to know his onions,' said Merril rolling a fag.

'I'm pretty sure the name of the Tibetan deity is Dorje Shugden,' said Barry.

'Mollie Sugden was in *Are You Being Served?* off the telly,' said Molly, 'I think the Oracle is a bit mental, bless him.'

Barry shrugged his shoulders, 'I'll find out the day after tomorrow, won't I?'

Molly seized hold of Barry's hands, her weary blue eyes fastening onto him.

'Are you actually gonna go?'

'Of course he is,' said Merril, blowing a plume of smoke upwards, 'and I'll be with him.'

'No, I'm going alone this time, this is a one-man ninja

mission. Dad trained me for this, and now is the time to stand up and be counted.'

Molly scrunched up her forehead and threw a teary glance at Merril.

'How about you just do surveillance this time, hey?' Merril put her arm around Molly. 'Study their movements, look for weak points, that kind of thing.'

'Why?'

'Once we have the right intelligence, we can hit 'em hard, can't we?'

'I suppose...'

'It does make sense, love,' said Molly, blowing her nose.

'Anyway, I'm Lee Marvin; fish supper anyone?'[5] Merril squeezed Barry's flabby biceps. 'It's my treat, we need to build your strength up.'

———————————

1. If I'm honest, I was bit wary of Barry going into this situation without me, but thankfully I was able to keep a close eye on him via my remote-viewing app. I can view events anywhere in the multiverse. Current astronomical theory would have you believe there are limitless parallel universes, but there are actually only two; ours, and another one that is slightly more crap. I know, I was disappointed too. Don't believe me? I'll prove it to you later.

2. Wanna hear something messed up? Later that night, when everyone had gone to bed. I broke into the Inner Sanctum for a spot of recon. I was having a sniff around when I heard someone coming, so I ducked behind the oracle's platform, and the strangest thing happened. Bertie Backwards came into the room, naked and quite clearly aroused. He drank from the Oracle's spittoon and then started a Morris dancing routine, waving the tea towel through the air. I was stuck there for two hours. I hate my job sometimes.

3. A 'Monkey' is Cockney slang meaning £500. This expression was taken from Indian currency, whose 500 rupee note had a monkey printed on it. The Brits borrowed a few other things from the Indian people, most notably their country.

4. Amphitheatre – part of the legacy of the Roman invasion. They equipped Britain with all kinds of useful things, including, it is said, central heating. If there are any Romans reading this, you couldn't pop round and help me drain my system, could you? Mine is open-vented with eight radiators, and the one in the upstairs bathroom is hardly

chucking out any heat at all. Do you know what I mean? I would do it myself, but the bleed valves are a bit fiddly. Cheers.

5. Lee Marvin was an American actor who starred in the classic film *The Dirty Dozen*. His name was incorporated into Cockney rhyming slang, meaning 'starving.' If you go on holiday to London, try using the phrase 'I'm well Lee Marvin, geezer.' It is particularly welcome in expensive hotels and restaurants.

Chapter Eleven

KNUCKLE BONES

Day 2 – 2 p.m.

Below ground, worms and insects chew up organic matter so they can poop out rich fertile humus that feeds the trees, which in turn provide the very air we breathe. It is a thriving ecological economy that works in harmony to support an exquisite eco-system on a planet that glides effortlessly, gracefully and eternally through infinite space.

Above ground, humans use their creative abilities to invent toxic chemicals that wipe out vast swathes of insects that we depend on for our survival. Luckily, there are still a few sensitive individuals left who work tirelessly to maintain the world's beauty and purity; selfless individuals acting from a place of compassion and kindness rather than greed or anger.

Barry was up on his allotment going through some of his most deadly ninja moves.

Ordinarily, a day on the allotment would mean double

digging, manure spreading, and potting seedlings for the season ahead. Today, however, was dedicated to revising his skill set—truth be told, he was a tad rusty. Contrary to popular opinion, Barry's dad Yamoshi had trained him in the art of ninjutsu daily from the age of six right up until his disappearance when Barry was twenty-five. These daily lessons took many forms. Sometimes they would be direct combat, other times they could take the form of a philosophical discussion about the nature of reality. Occasionally, Yamoshi would spring a *koan* on Barry—a seemingly unanswerable riddle devised to create deeper insights. The *koan* that had stuck in Barry's mind the longest was, 'What is the sound of one hand clapping?' Barry strained his brain and tried his best, but the only insight he ever derived from them was one of those migraines that feel like needles are being inserted into the backs of your eyes.

He hadn't been sleeping at all well. It had been 3 years now, and not having his father around had placed a heavy burden on his shoulders. He wanted more than anything to step up and fill his dad's shoes, but now the moment had arrived, he felt like he was wading through quicksand wearing an old-fashioned diving suit. Luckily, one of the benefits of not being in touch with your feelings is that you are less bothered by them, if you notice them at all, and Barry was nothing if not stubborn. He slipped on his silk kimono and tied his ninja mask tight around his head. His heart raced as he started his warm-up exercises, and a sickly bile rose in his throat as he threw fast punches into the cool spring air. The sweet aroma of freshly-cultivated soil filled his nostrils as he kicked over the remaining stalks of last year's kale, then transitioned into a flying kick over the garlic bed. This was just the ticket to use up the excess cortisone swirling round his system. Just as he was starting to feel empowered, the image of a samurai's gigantic curved sword popped into his mind, blade glistening in the sunlight like a rare jewel, deadlier than a king cobra.

How the hell can I defend myself against one of those?

Sensing somebody breathing behind him, Barry spun around, ready for action, only to find his neighbour Brian, gawping at him.

'Afternoon,' said Brian, putting down his bag. 'Having fun?'

'Not exactly,' puffed Barry.

'This isn't connected with the cinema massacre, is it?'

'Yeah, I'm planning on going out in style.' Barry bent forward to work on his hamstrings.

'They said on the news that the police still haven't found them. They're getting the army in to organise a manhunt.'

'Until that happens, it's me against three psycho samurai. What do you reckon of my odds?'

'I'm no gambling man, but I know there's many paths up Ben Nevis.' Brian pointed his finger meaningfully in the direction of Scotland.

'There's only two paths up Ben Nevis,' replied Barry

'OK, you know what I mean though.'

'No.'

'Come on, you do.'

'Nope.'

In order to elaborate, Brian nestled onto his favourite perch on the boundary fence while Barry adopted the look of a man trapped in a broken down lift with the cast of *The Hills Have Eyes*.

'When I was a nipper, there was a game we used to play called Knuckle Bones. We used to collect old tin cans and play tunes on them with hollow animal bones we found round the back of the slaughter yard up on Mr Bigby's farm.'

'Health and safety has come a long way.' said Barry.

'We used to put on a big show in the square outside Mrs

Carter's sweet shop. Everyone came out to watch, including Mrs Carter. The distraction gave one of our gang the opportunity to sneak into the shop and pilfer bags of sweets.'

'The whole thing was a ruse?'

'Exactly,' said Brian, straightening his shirt cuffs. 'It was perfectly executed sweet larceny. The plan worked flawlessly for months, until our first day back at school. My mum always bought me school trousers that were too big so I wouldn't outgrow them. We put on a show after school, and having stuffed my pockets with sweets, my trousers fell down as I was making my getaway. I tripped over and knocked myself out. Mrs Carter found me lying in the doorway with my trousers round my ankles and flying saucers everywhere.'[1]

'Karma,' Barry smirked. 'So what's this got to do with me?'

'Present your enemy with a spectacle, not a threat. Put them at ease, and you may find your chance.'

'You know these guys are seven feet tall, right?'

'The harder they fall, Barry, the harder they fall.'

'A long as they don't fall on me, hey?' said Barry, shrugging off his kimono and stuffing it into his backpack.

'You know, I'd love to help.' Brian puffed out his chest. 'But my sciatica has really been playing me up lately. I'll be with you in spirit, comrade.'

'Thanks, comrade.' Barry strapped his backpack on and made ready to leave.

Trotting over to get something from his shed and turning on his heel towards Barry, Brian handed him a dirty old spray bottle with a faded label. 'Here's a little something to take with you.'

'What's in it?'

'100% DDT, the most toxic pesticide ever invented. This little baby could bring a herd of stampeding buffalo to their knees. It's essentially a weapon of mass destruction, banned in the 70s due to the carnage it was causing. When they announced the ban, I stocked up my shed; it's the only thing that gets rid of knotweed.' Brian settled back onto the fence. 'I know an interesting anecdote about that, actually...'

Barry took the bottle and scurried home, leaving Brian to wax lyrical to his onion patch. When he got back, he found Molly and Merril sat at the kitchen table devouring a packet of chocolate Hobnobs.

'I could eat a whale,' said Molly, licking every last morsel from her fingers.

Merril gave Barry a faint smile, and struggling to keep her eyes open, returned her attention back to Molly, 'How did it go at the market?'

'Nuffin' at all, I asked everyone.'

'Same in town, I'm gonna talk to her workmates tomorrow.'

Barry managed to grab the last Hobnob before Molly got to it. 'I hope I can dig something up, Ril.'

'Remember, it's just surveillance.' Molly pointed an unsteady finger at Barry.

'I know, I know.' Walking over to the window, Barry looked up at the beetroot sky, a burning in the pit of his stomach. He knew tomorrow would be a full moon, but he had no clue what horror would await him. One thing was clear, though; surveillance would not be an option.

---

1. Not real flying saucers of course. These are little UFO shaped capsules made of rice paper and filled with sherbet. They were recently voted Britain's favourite sweets of all time, which I can only assume is part of larger conspiracy to downgrade the validity of life from other planets. That said, I stopped travelling in flying saucers years ago. With the progress teleportation has made, it is no longer necessary. I do occasionally fly over small villages in Belgium in a spaceship, but that's just for a laugh.

Chapter Twelve

A ROMAN CANDLE

Day 3 – 7 a.m.

Having just drop-kicked the living daylights out of hundreds of trashy news reporters, blown up the offices of their vile gutter press, and then single-handedly rescued a dozen glamour models from a life of exploitation and servitude, the last thing Barry needed was someone banging on his front door and waking him up.

He wiped the drool from his face, hung his barnacled feet over the side of the bed, and attempted to get his head together as the knocks resounded again. *Bang, bang, bang!*

What the hell's going on? Is it those psychopaths again? No, can't be...they wouldn't knock. Barry crept softly to the front door in nothing but his Batman underpants and peered through the spyglass. It was Mrs Caswell from the Portslade Bowls Society, looking like she had been up all night drinking fermented urine.

'Mr Harris, are you in there? I have a furious bowls team

out here who want some answers. Mr Tilbury tripped on a divot and broke his ankle just as he was about to take the winning shot. I think you have some explaining to do, don't you?'

Barry hurried down the hallway into Molly's bedroom.

'Mum, Mum! Get up, get up, I need some help!'

Molly fell out of bed with her nightie hitched into the back of her knickers. 'What the bloody hell have you done this time?' she blurted, straightening herself out.

'It's the bowls team, they lost their tournament and they're blaming me for some reason. Do you know what a divot is?'

'It's one of them puffy blankets posh people use,' said Molly, holding her head in her hands. *Bang, bang, bang!* 'The cheeky fuckers, they can't come round to my house and do this, it's seven o'clock in the bleedin' morning! You get out of the bathroom window, and I'll give 'em a piece of my mind.' Molly stormed off to the front door.

Barry ran back to his room, pulled on his dressing gown, shimmied through the bathroom window and cautiously made his way down the drainpipe as Molly took the fight to the bowls team. As he did, the flimsy fastener fell off his dressing gown, causing it to flap in the sea breeze like a cape. From a distance, he might have looked like the caped crusader.[1] Halfway down, he stopped to look around to make sure no stray members of the bowls club had clocked him. He noticed Dr Harper standing at the bus stop, staring up at him.

'Morning Barry, everything OK?'

'Not really, Mrs Caswell's after me.'

'Ah, I see. I really must change her medication,' the doctor mumbled to himself. 'Do you need any more help? You look like you are on another adventure!' The doctor's eyes glistened as he puffed animatedly on his pipe.

'A rather upset bowls team will be appearing soon, would you be able to distract them while I do a runner?'

'Don't worry, Barry, I know just the thing. I saw it in a film, it can't fail.' The doctor buttoned up his tweed jacket and readied himself.

When Barry reached *terra firma*, he turned around to find next door's dog, Keith looking up at him. He was covered in mud, and the previously buried hand lay on the lawn in front of him.

'Nice underpants,' said Keith.

Silence.

'I wanted to get a cape, but it's not dog appropriate, *apparently*.'

More silence.

'Going somewhere in a hurry? You'll catch your death out here like that.'

'Uh...are you *speaking* to me?' asked Barry.

'Yep,' said Keith, wiping his paws on the lawn. 'Do we really need to do the whole "dogs can't talk" thing? Obviously I can, so can you just get your head round it?'

'Er...OK, so who...are you?' Barry rubbed his eyes to confirm he was awake, but wished he could just go back to his dream.

'That's a Pandora's Box you don't want to open, man, trust me. Let's keep it simple for now. In layman's terms, I'm Keith, an inter-dimensional Basset Hound who is able to co-exist within both dimensions of the multi-verse, as well as in all possible iterations of the past and future.'[2]

Barry opened his mouth to speak but realised he had nothing to say. His only contribution was a rivulet of drool which torrented enthusiastically down his stubbly chin.

Keith raised his eyebrows and continued, 'The job description sounds impressive until you realise I have to spend most of my time looking after idiots like you. We'd better get a move on.'

'Look after me? What are you talking ab—'

'There's no time, you have a midday appointment at the vortex, don't you?'

'The vortex? You mean the amphitheatre? How did you—'

At that moment, Mrs Caswell stepped away from the front door and into the front garden.

'There he is, get him!'

Twenty members of the bowls team came charging down the stairs waving an assortment of gardening tools. There was something about their demeanour that indicated to Barry that they weren't planning on helping him with the weeding.

'Run!' shouted Keith, disappearing through the front gate. 'Follow me!'

Barry ran onto the High Street, trying to look as inconspicuous as he could whilst being chased by a gang of marauding OAPs, wearing Batman underpants, and talking to a Basset Hound. The wrinkly agitators came flooding out of Barry's garden to find Dr Harper lying in wait. Pumped to the max and ready for anything, he threw himself at Mrs Caswell's, feet clutching his chest.

'Help! I'm having a heart attack!'

Without batting an eyelid, Mrs Caswell stepped over him and carried on in pursuit of Barry and Keith as they entered the park gates on the other side of the road.

'The Oracle said they will be at the old amphitheatre at the back of the park,' said Barry.

'He's no oracle,' Keith panted as he took a shortcut through a bed of particularly attractive delphiniums.

'How did he know all that stuff, then?' said Barry, struggling to keep up.

'I told him. What time is it?'

'8 a.m.'

'If we have *any* chance of gaining an advantage, we had better hurry; the fourth dimension exchange windows are only open till midday.'

'What the—?'

Keith sped ahead like a panther, his big velvety ears flapping in the wind.

Feeling like the contents of his stomach were trying to make their way up his windpipe, Barry was forced to stop and catch his breath, though not for long, as he could see an army of white jumpers doddering towards him. He quickly set off again, taking a route behind some overgrown hedgerows until he arrived at the edge of the amphitheatre, where he found Keith etching a series of calculations into the ground with his paws. His collar had orange lights oscillating backwards and forwards on it, and a voice echoed from a small built-in speaker.

'This is an automated reminder from the Prophecy Allocation Department. You have thirty minutes remaining to register a fourth-dimension exchange window.'[3]

'We're running out of time.' Keith paced up and down, jabbing at a green flashing button on his collar with a paw.

Barry slumped to the ground next to him, his heart whirring.

The amphitheatre is an impressive structure. Built around 400 CE, it was designed by the Romans and built for an emperor. It is now mainly used by the Portslade Amateur Dramatic society for their yearly performance of *The Wizard of Oz*. The lowest point of the amphitheatre is fifty meters below ground level, and its stone seating is divided into wedge shapes punctuated by thin passageways running from the highest point down to a wall surrounding the arena. On either side of the arena, two exits known as *vomitoria* were cut into the chalk bedrock. Originally, gladiators would enter from one side and wild beasts from the other, and the emperor would sit and lord it over the oppressed masses from a large platform above the gladiator's entrance.

'Where shall we hide?' asked Barry, wiping the sweat out of his eyes.

'Right where they can see us,' replied Keith. 'Follow me, I've got a plan.' With that, he scampered down one of the passageways, through the nettles, and hopped up onto the emperor's marble podium. Barry clambered on behind him and started strutting round the platform with his hands on his hips and his chest puffed out, peering down his nose at the imagined plebeians in the audience.

'What are you doing, you knob?' Keith shook his head. 'I think you'd better look upwards.'

Barry looked up to see the OAPs surrounding the perimeter of the amphitheatre. As one, they started banging their weapons against the stone seats as though in some apocalyptic gangland stand-off.

'They're trying to get into our heads!' Keith shouted over the deafening noise.

The ageing gangsters slowly made their way towards the arena, Mrs Caswell leading the way. Who'd have thought it, an eighty-four-year-old woman who, on any other day, would be busying herself with account sheets and crumpets, was baying for justice, justice that could only be delivered with Barry's blood.

'We need to buy some time until the samurai show up,' said Keith, sniffing the air for the latest updates. 'I need you to jump down into the arena and lure them in toward you.'

'You must be fucking joking, they'll skin me alive!'

'Don't worry. It's my job to protect you.'

'No offence mate, but you are a *Basset Hound*.'[4]

'None taken.' With that, Keith jumped up and knocked Barry backwards off the emperor's platform, slamming him down onto the muddy floor of the arena.'

'Keith, you bastard!' Barry dug mud out of his ear, his head ringing.

'Trust me,' shouted Keith, 'just trust me.'

Seeing Barry fall, the mob started climbing down the arena's inner wall.

'Let me take the first swing,' came a voice from the back of the horde, 'the little bastard!'

Barry jumped to his feet and tried scrambling back up the wall onto the platform, but there was no time and he was soon surrounded. A hand grabbed him by the scruff off his neck and thrust him against the wall.

'Hold your horses, Batman.' Mrs Caswell's head rocked like a child's bobble-headed figurine. 'It seems we have you cornered, don't we? You have a choice; either you do what I say, or I let this lot get their way.'

'What do I have to do?'

'You are going to pay for the bowls clubhouse to be completely refurbished, the greens returfed, and, and as a gesture of good will and penitence, you will pay a generous convalescence stipend to Mr Tilbury.'

'That sounds reasonable,' Barry wrinkled his nose. 'How much would that little lot set me back then?'

'£75,000 should do it.'

Despite the situation, he couldn't contain himself. 'Ha ha! That is never gonna happen, grandma. I am currently over-drawn to the tune of forty-eight quid and sixty-three pence.' Though he was never any good at making or holding onto money, Barry always knew how much he *didn't* have.

'Don't say I didn't give you the chance. Get him, boys and girls.' Mrs Caswell raised her arm to signal the assault, but then held it aloft, arrested mid-signal, as she noticed a dense fog flooding down the passageways into the arena. On the far side, three dark figures stepped out of the *vomitoria*.

'Who the *hell* are they?' cried Mrs Caswell. The figures raised their swords in the air, seeming to mock Mrs Caswell's still-raised-but-swordless arm. The sun ricocheted from their razor-sharp blades in kaleidoscopic fashion, piercing the wispy fog.

'I'm not sure you want to mess with those guys.' said Barry

'Oh really? I think we can see off a few idiots in fancy dress. Charge!'

'Keith,' called Barry, 'it's round about now you need to get your act together mate!'

Keith plodded over to the edge of the platform and placed his two front paws on top of the wall to anchor himself. Using his nose, he pushed a metal flick-switch on his collar that whirred as a long thin metal wire extended down into the arena.

'Grab that!' shouted Keith as he nosed the switch again. Barry was pulled upwards onto the emperor's platform. By the time he had righted himself, Keith was sat watching a 3D holographic film being projected from his collar by a small camera. Various images from the history of the universe were being played out in quick succession.

'What the hell is that?'

'It's a cosmic possibility tracer. I invented it.'

'There's a massacre kicking off down there! I can see Mr Pippin the club secretary's head being manually removed from his shoulders; is this the best time to be watching a documentary?'

'It's a visual representation of events that have occurred in this locale since the dawn of creation,' Keith explained nonchalantly. 'When an opportune event from the past or the future falls into the tracer's sequencing coordinates, I have the ability to create an exchange window that swaps that time frame for the present. The whole thing lasts about thirty seconds, and is confined to just this location. Good, hey?'

'You expect me to believe that?'

Keith sighed heavily as Barry looked down to see the warriors slicing through the remainder of the bowls team, who were now desperately trying to escape down the *vomitoria*.

'Whatever you're gonna do, just hurry up,' urged Barry. 'The samurai are making their way over to us!'

'We're almost there, we'll be ready...anytime...now!' Keith nose-tapped another button on his collar, and with a candescent flash reminiscent of Molly's cooking, the entire arena was instantly filled with Roman gladiators, rhinos, tigers and elephants rampaging with anarchic abandon.

'What the—?' Barry couldn't believe his eyes.

Keith's ears danced on his head as he jumped up and down. 'It worked! We've gone back to 400 CE.'

Just then, a rhino charged into the middle of the remaining bowls team, sending them flying, and the gladiators surrounded the samurais, who, somewhat dumbfounded, grasped their swords and engaged in fierce and bloody battle.

Ramming head-first into the arena wall, an African bush elephant brought down the front section of the emperor's platform, then reared up on his stumpy hind legs to prepare himself for another attack.

'We can't take another hit,' said Keith. 'We'll end up in the arena. Quick, take my coll—'

'Wait, I wanna see who wins between the samurai and the gladiators! This is *better* than Star Trek.'

'You are such a dick!' Keith headbutted Barry in the shins. 'Press the red button on the back of my collar three times, then run like hell!' Barry completed his task and sprinted after Keith as they hopped off the platform and scuttled up the passageway. Turning to look behind him, Barry saw a tornado appear, sucking the inhabitants of the arena into a raging torrent in its centre. Just before the feisty duo could reach the top of the amphitheatre, another flash blazed and they were blown sky-high, legs flailing. Keith was drawn backwards towards the arena, and Barry hit the ground hard, landing face-first before coming to lie as still and silent as the stone seats that surrounded him.

---

1. If he didn't have such a fat arse.
2. Let me be clear here, this Basset Hound is, in the words of my American boss, the shit. Of course dogs can talk (except Whippets). Pugs have really weird accents, and Chow Chows do not need to speak, as they are telepathic for some reason. Poodles are generally right wing wankers, so are best avoided.
3. You know I said the multiverse only has two dimensions? The Prophecy Allocation Department links them both together. Essentially, it is an office block at a crossroads between the seen and the unseen worlds. The Department owns the fabric of existence, and they control everything within it. Yes, I'm afraid that means free will is an illusion, albeit a necessary one, and everything you do, see, and touch is being manipulated by a stuffy administrator for the sake of an intergalactic experiment. I hope this doesn't spoil your enjoyment of the rest of your life.
4. Once again, we see the marginalisation of the canine community. It's all human this, human that with you lot, isn't it? Things may change one day...

DR PLEASURE

Day 3 – 7 a.m.

O nce a month, Dr Harper sets his alarm two hours early and, taking care not to wake his wife, leaves his home to embark on a clandestine trip to the Portslade Pleasure Factory.

Given that the establishment is tucked away down so many backstreets, he can make the journey and be fairly confident that none of his patients will see him. Well, providing they aren't visiting the establishment themselves, of course—though even this eventuality has been guarded against. Due to the customers' need for discretion, there are private viewing rooms at the rear of the factory that allow the more sensitive clientele to peruse the Factory's wares to their hearts' content without being rumbled. Each client is given a code to the security door so they can come and go as they please, and pre-booked appointments ensure there are no embarrassing encounters upon arrival or departure.

The doctor had availed himself of this arrangement countless times before this particular occasion, becoming very friendly with Jefferey on account of their shared love of dominos, making model aeroplanes, and watching hard-core transgender pornography.[1]

Running later than usual, the doctor let himself in, poured himself a steaming cup of coffee from his flask, and was soon entranced by the waxy, wipe-clean pages of the new arrivals catalogue. The synapses in the doctor's brain lit up like an aerial view of Las Vegas by night. As he sat pondering how much he could get away with spending without raising any suspicion, he couldn't help becoming aware of a loud commotion from the shop floor. This was most unusual for the time of morning, as the staff weren't due in for at least another hour. He managed to tear himself away from his book of shiny new things and walked over to the peephole in the door that looked out across the shop floor. Display cabinets were falling like dominoes, their glass panels smashing as Merril was dragged through the aisles by the same horned samurai warrior that had trapped Barry up the tree, though this time he was minus Mrs Hill's leg. The doctor quietly turned the latch and peeled open the door just wide enough. As you would expect, Merril wasn't going quietly, grabbing out for anything she could get her hands on and throwing it at the warrior.

'Let me get to my feet, you knobhead,' screamed Merril. 'Just give me the chance.' The samurai stared at her stony-faced, shook his head, and carried on.

'Where's my niece? If you've laid a finger on her, God help me I will take you down.'

The doctor sneaked out of the room and hid behind a display counter to get a closer look.

Opening the door to the storage room that had been Jo's prison cell for the past two days, the samurai released the smell of death onto the shop floor. Jo was still lying face down on top of Jeffrey's cold, stiff body. Merril screamed as her eyes fell on her niece, and she shook free of the warrior's grip and threw a barrage of her hardest punches into his iron ribs. She punched until blood gushed from her scrawny knuckles.

'I'll bleedin' kill you!'

The warrior stood before her like a rock, as remorseless as the nearby mannequins in the BDSM aisle.[2] He picked her up with one hand and launched her into the room so she landed slap-bang on top of Jo and Jeffery's static bodies.

Shocked by what he had witnessed, the doctor turned to make his escape and ran directly into the vibrator counter, sending all manner of contraptions bouncing across the parquet floor. Picking himself up amidst a sea of quivering 15-inch love probes, the doctor hoped beyond all hope that maybe there was a chance he hadn't been heard. Cautiously, he peered over the counter, and met his own reflection in the polished steel of a samurai sword.

---

1. After Jeffrey's demise, one of the UK's most loved drag queens, 'Domino-trix' was mysteriously never seen again. It's always the quiet ones hey? Everyone has their secrets, I suppose. I bet you do.

2. To be fair, the samurai wasn't wearing nipple clamps or a PVC dog collar with the words '*Spank Me*' emblazoned across it. Samurais do wear these nappy type things though, which is a *bit* kinky. Just saying.

Chapter Fourteen

BETWEEN WORLDS

Day 3 – 5 p.m.

Barry opened his eyes to find himself staring directly into Mrs Caswell's face. Unfortunately, the rest of her was nowhere to be seen. He tried to move, but realised he was planted firmly into a muddy verge at the top of the amphitheatre like some weird human-vegetable cultivar. There was a chilling calm in the air; a silence that gave no clue to the carnage that had recently unfolded. The upside-down world that Barry now found himself in had very little left that could surprise him—or so he thought.

He burrowed, scratched and scraped, attempting to haul his body free, but was so firmly lodged that he gave up, panting. Two more heroic attempts later, Barry finally stood vertically, and his thoughts turned to Jo.

Please make today the day I find her.

He peeled his mud-encrusted fringe from his forehead, picked up Mrs Caswell's face as a memento, and trudged off in search of Keith. As he descended toward the arena, the smell of raw meat clawed at the back of Barry's throat. Shreds of bloodied bowling club jumpers lay strewn across the arena floor in a circular pattern, like a demonic mandala.

'Keith, where are you?'

'Arrrgh.' A groan could be heard from the other side of the amphitheatre. Using his finely tuned sixth sense, Barry traced the noise to a pile of body parts strewn amongst the weeds. He uncovered poor old Keith, who laid arse to the heavens, covered in the tell-tale red blotches of nettle stings.[1]

'I'm raw as hell.' Keith tried to navigate himself into a more dignified pose.

'We need to find some dock leaves.' Barry surveyed the terrain.

'Come near me with one of those, and I'll bite your hand off.'

'Alright, keep your floppy ears on.' Barry sat down beside Keith and grinned. 'Wanna see what I've got?' He whipped Mrs Caswell's face out, stretching it lengthwise. 'Oh, why the long face?'

Keith shook his head and rolled over onto his tender paws.

'Ow...just so you know, you are by far the biggest idiot I've ever been assigned to.'

'I'll take that at face value,' replied Barry, beaming.

Keith, unable to find the right words, merely licked at his sore spots.

'I better put this down now, it's getting hard to keep a straight face.'

Tutting to himself, Keith peered over the arena wall. 'I was lucky not to get sucked into the vortex, you know. I stuck my leg through a hole in the wall and managed to hold on by sheer paw-power.'[2]

'What did your collar do?'

'It was just your standard vortex implosion time swap,' replied Keith, shrugging. 'It's pretty basic stuff; I'll be surprised if the samurai got taken all the way back to ancient Greece, but it does buy us some time, especially if they get lost in the deserts of the Before and After.'[3]

Barry looked confused but remembered his mission. 'We need to get a move on and find Jo, it's been three days. Time has nearly run out.'

As they made their way back up the blood-splattered steps, Keith was struck by a curious scene in the middle of the arena. What looked like a pair of feet stuck directly upright out of the soil.

'How peculiar,' he mumbled, wrinkling his forehead. 'I'm feeling the urge to investigate.'

'There's no time, finding Jo is the number one priority!'

Keith, however, had already scampered back down the steps. Barry followed reluctantly, and they waded through the carnage until they arrived at the legs, which were adorned with cream-coloured woollen tights and a pair of the brown zip boots that older ladies tend to wear. Keith shook his head, his ears fluttering in the cool sea breeze that was starting to blow in. 'The gateway must have closed before she had the chance to cross over. The sad thing is, she's probably still alive...somewhere.'

'I think I know who it is,' said Barry, his eyes moistening. 'It's dear old Mrs Garrett from Bunty's Bakery. She's the only person in Portslade to have pictures of Eccles cakes[4] embroidered onto her tights.'

Keith sniffed the ground, and his eyes narrowed as he screwed up his face. 'I wonder if...' He shook his head and drifted back into his thoughts.

'She used to give Mum a free doughnut for me every

morning when I was a kid,' said Barry. 'She was the main reason behind my acne explosion; lovely lady though. Now look at her. That's what happens when you fall in with the wrong crowd, I suppose.'

'Where's her head at?' asked Keith.

'Exactly.'

'No, I mean literally, where's her head at?'

'Oh, I see. Can't we try and pull her out?'

'No way.' Keith held up a paw and shook it dismissively. 'It would completely dislodge her psychic circuitry. One day she would think she was in Portslade, the next in ancient Rome. That is, unless...' Keith pressed a small, hitherto unused button on his collar. A virtual whiteboard appeared in front of him, onto to which he started to scribble a series of mathematical equations with a paw. 'There is a possibility that, because she was the last to go in, she didn't make it all the way back to Rome, in which case, it is very likely the top half of her body is sticking up in the Before and After, the place we refer to in the business as 'between worlds'. If my sums are correct, it is also the most likely place our three friends would try and evade the time swap.'

'It's getting late, Keith; how is this helping Jo?'

'If we can find a way to communicate with Mrs Garrett, she may have some vital clues to help us defeat this enemy.'

'But how?'

'That's what I've been trying to figure out, idiot. We've only got access from her feet up to her hips...but if we can find some way to form a feedback loop within her, we just might be able to communicate.'

'What if...' Barry paused to stare meaningfully at the sky, 'we pull up some of the park's irrigation pipe and try to thread it down her tights to reach the top half of her body?'

'That won't work. Although Mrs Garrett is in effect one entity, within the four-dimensional space-time continuum, she is two halves of the same person caught in a two-way fractal schism.'[5]

'If only she had a pair of ears and a mouth on her knees, hey?'

Keith flung his head back, sending the saggy skin round his mouth bouncing in all directions. 'You mean set up an internal quantum conduit using the four-dimensional crystal lattice principle, transmitted via a form of virtual sound card?'

Barry nodded his head slowly with pursed lips. 'Yeah... that's what I meant.'

'That's the best idea I've heard in a long time. Maybe you're not such an idiot.'

Barry proudly fastened the belt on his dressing gown. Perhaps even *he* didn't realise the depths of his own talent. It was unlikely, though.

'It will take a bit of weird science,' said Keith, 'but I did try it on my brother who got stuck down a rabbit hole once. I will clone my own ears and mouth and then fuse them to Mrs Garrett's knees and hip.' Keith busied himself with preparations, pressing more buttons on his collar until a green laser began printing perfect replicas of his sensory organs. As soon as they were finished, Barry picked up the ears and dangled them by the sides of his head.

'They're all wet, what are they made of?'

'Vulcanized rubber,' said Keith, 'I have to file a special request to print in flesh, there's just no time.' Keith held the ears against Mr's Garrett's knees, carefully adjusting them so they were equidistant. 'Hold them just here, I need to meld them together with my homonuclear diatomic fuser.'[6] Keith pressed a glowing white button on his collar, which produced a pulsating heat wave. So intense was the smell of burning flesh, Barry started to retch. Once the ears had been fused, it was time to join the replica mouth to Mrs Garrett's hip.

When it was done, Keith stepped back to admire his handiwork. 'I'm worried it's not going to work.'

'Well, she can always use the ears as knee warmers,' said Barry, winking.

Keith ignored the comment.

'Or kneeling cushions when she's gardening,'

'Shut up. Let's test this out.' Keith got up on two paws and spoke as clearly as he could into the rubber ears. 'Can you hear me, Mrs Garrett?'

No response.

'Is anyone there?'

Nothing.

'Just as I feared, there's not enough bio-quantum inter-dimensional signal-to-noise volition.' Keith did some more sums whilst muttering to himself. 'If we can form some kind of vibrational sound loop, we may be able to use my advanced sonaric echolalia technology to boost the sound transmission...'

Barry nodded, whilst shrugging his shoulders as if to say 'surely that was obvious?' The sea breeze picked up, and the temperature began falling rapidly. Barry scooped up the shredded remains of a bowls jumper and hoisted it onto his shoulders. A cursory glance revealed it was smeared in something that looked suspiciously like brains, so Barry just didn't look.

If you can't see it, it's not there.

'Hey, genius, go and get me some of that irrigation pipe you mentioned, there's one thing more we can try.' Barry scampered up the hill like a good human obeying his canine master[7] while Keith pressed a small pink button on his collar to produce his 3D sonar.

Ten minutes later, dripping wet and with the face the colour of beetroot, Barry reappeared holding an armful of the park's irrigation system.

'I need you to put one end in the ear on the right knee and the other in the mouth on her hip.' Keith fiddled manically with the settings. The words *'Application Configuration in Progress'* appeared on the 3D screen, along with a familiar-looking progress bar. All of a sudden, a cacophony of forest noises could be heard loud and clear; there were cicadas, shrieking monkeys, bird calls, and running water alongside what appeared to be the agitated voices of the samurai.

'Where's all that noise coming from?' asked Barry.

'I've just turned Mrs Garrett's backside into a tannoy system,' said Keith. 'It's a little undignified, I suppose, but it's the only option we had left. It could save her life.'

Keith was about to speak again when Mrs Garrett's buttocks interjected. 'Hello? Is...is someone there?'

Barry quickly knelt down, then paused for a moment before looking back at Keith and whispering, 'Do I speak to her butt or your ears?'

Keith pointed wearily at the ears.

'Mrs Garrett, it's me, Barry Harris, where are you?'

'Oh Barry, help me! I'm in some kind of forest.'

'That'll be the Forest of Fabulous Abundance and Pitiful Remorse,' mumbled Keith.[8]

'It's all very strange. The samurai gentlemen, they keep asking questions...they are coming back again now!'

'What you know about Prophecy, old lady?' Screamed the samurai with the bullhorns.

'I don't understand, dear.'

'What special powers does Barry Harris have?'

'He's a gardener, if that's what you mean.'

'Are you a witch, old lady?'

'I work in a cake shop on the high street.'

Barry nudged Keith, 'What the hell is he talking about? A Prophecy?'

Keith looked at him with a furrowed brow. 'Ask her to find out where they are hiding Jo.'

Without warning, the signal went dead, replaced by the white noise of a poorly tuned radio. Mrs Garrett's legs toppled over and landed with a thud on the ground. Barry turned to Keith. 'Shall I get more hosepipe?'

'No, it can only mean one thing.'

'What?'

'She's been chopped in half.'

'The bastards!' Barry punched the ground. 'I'm gonna make them pay!'

Keith stared pensively at the blood splattered Eccles cakes on Mrs Garrett's tights. 'I've never seen anything like these warriors before; I don't know how we are going to beat them. We may be forced into using the last resort.'

'Last resort?'

Keith ignored the response, shook himself down, and scampered out of the arena. Barry trudged behind with clenched fists and a racing heart. As they got to the top of the amphitheatre, they looked back at the arena one last time.

'There will be some very confused police in this town,' said Keith. 'Even I'm struggling to make sense of it. At least one good thing has come out of it.'

'Which is?' asked Barry.

'You'll never have to do the bowls club job again.'

Barry gave him the faintest of smiles.

'Before we part ways, I couldn't ask you a favour by any chance?'

'What?' Barry couldn't imagine what incomprehensible task it might be.

'You couldn't just scratch my back, could you?' begged Keith, trying to point to it and nearly toppling over. 'There's a spot just by my tail—'[9]

'There's no time!'

'Quite right, but you can't blame a dog for asking. Anyway, I'd better split, I've got an appointment with the boss and she hates me being late.'

'For God's sake!' said Barry, losing it. 'Who is your boss?'

'Are you sure you don't know?' said Keith, raising his eyebrows. 'Let's just say we have a mutual acquaintance.' With that, Keith disappeared into the undergrowth leaving Barry alone, confused, and so utterly exhausted he could hardly see straight.

He pointed himself in the direction of Portslade High Street and leant forward, just about managing to put one foot in front of the other. The one thing propelling him forward was the thought of seeing Molly's smiling face when he got home, but an enormous plate of fish fingers wouldn't go amiss. And Jo. God, Jo!

---

1. The sheer humiliation.
2. So very brave...and strong.
3. The Before and After refers to an in-between realm of the multiverse, first mentioned in the intricate world building of *Escape from Samsara*, Book One of The Prophecy Allocation Series. If you haven't read it, do so now...well, either after reading this or at the same time, by contacting yourself in a parallel universe.

   Looks like we've arrived back at the 'Many Worlds' theory of quantum mechanics again. What would you say if you had the chance to meet yourself in person? The first time, I did I said, 'Stop writing such puerile nonsense and try for a literary classic.' I replied to myself with my typical erudite charm by saying 'Oh, piss off!'. In doing so, I unwittingly undermined the idea that I am capable of writing a classic, and this led to a cosmic epiphany in which I become one with my other self. Although we still exist within separate universes, we now plan to co-author 'saucy sci-fi' (yes, that is the market we're aiming for) for all eternity. Maybe that's what being 'at one' with yourself means, to collect all other versions of you in existence. I think I might have actually stumbled upon the meaning of life here! If that's not a literary classic, I don't know what is.
4. Eccles cakes are smallish round cakes covered in sugar and packed with

currants. They are the confectionary equivalent of crack cocaine. I'm not supposed to eat them, but I can't stop myself. I cover them in special margarine first so I don't die.

5. ...and clever.
6. Disclaimer: All the complex science and technology referred to in this story comes from another universe, so if you don't understand something, it is technically your fault. By the way, have you worked out who I am yet?
7. As it should be.
8. Places in the 'Before and After' are named as such, and are domains of sinister trickery and sticky misfortune. If you ever find yourself lost inside time and space and happen to come across them, run. Run for your life! Poor old Mrs Garrett can't do that though, can she? Bless her.
9. For all you Mensa candidates that haven't managed to work out who I am yet, *woof* you like me to give you a clue? Yes, it's me, Keith, your brave, strong and intelligent hero. I hope you are enjoying yourself. I wasn't planning on writing this story, but Barry wanted to do it, and we couldn't let that happen could we? It's hard writing about yourself, so I hope you appreciate my impartiality.

I have written a few self-help best sellers before, including *How to Roll in Horse Poop and Make it Look Like an Accident*. It's not really aimed at the human market, that one, but you might like, *Silent But Deadly: How to Clear a Dinner Party and Reclaim the Sofa in Under 30 Seconds.*'

Chapter Fifteen

MISSING PERSONS

Day 3 – roughly 11 p.m.

B arry chipped off the last of the paint surrounding the keyhole trying to get into his front door. He lay in the hallway for five minutes before somehow finding the energy to clamber up the stairs to the family home. Staggering into the kitchen, he wrangled a bumper bag of budget fish fingers out of the densely-packed freezer, in the process managing to send a packet of peas all over the kitchen floor. As he looked down, he realised the floor was also covered in Molly's whiskey-and-cola humbugs. He bolted into the front room to see it had been completely ransacked. Everything was either broken or upside down, and all the family pictures had been torn from the walls and lay smashed on the carpet.

'Mum, are you here? Mum?' Barry ran into Molly's bedroom, but there was no sign of her. He picked up the phone, finding it was covered in blood. His chest started pounding as he desperately dialled Merril's number. It rang and rang, and his galloping heart felt like it was going to give out any moment. There was no response. Not knowing what else to do next, he dialled that little number three times: 9⁻9⁻9.

'You are through to police emergencies. What is the nature of your emergency?'

'I want to report a kidnap.'

'Can you tell me who has been kidnapped, Sir?'

'It's my mum, Molly Harris.'

'Is this Barry Harris?'

'Yeah.'

'Didn't you report your father and sister missing recently as well?'

'Yes, but this is different. I don't think it's the same kidnappers.'

'Do you know who has taken your mother?'

'Yes. I mean, no—'

'Which is it, Sir?'

Barry dropped the phone and collapsed on Molly's bed, tears cascading down his face.

What's the point? They would never believe me.

On Molly's bedside cabinet sat a vase that looked like it had been created by Salvador Dali during his apprenticeship.[1] Barry scooped it up and hugged it as tight as he could. He watched as his tears ran down the side of it, giving it a much-needed glazed effect.

If there was ever a moment when I needed you, Dad, it is now...If only you could be here for ten minutes...just ten minutes. The grief and exhaustion combined to form an intoxicating sedative, but Barry fought it. *I mustn't sleep.* He struggled to his feet, flung open the bedroom window, and sat on the ledge, fighting to keep his eyes open.

As he inhaled the bitter night air, hopelessness engulfed him.

What if I just let myself fall? Put an end to all this…

He held the possibility in his mind for a few moments, wondering if he had the courage to act on it. The air stung his eyes and shivers darted through his body as he put his legs out of the window, balancing precariously on the wooden ledge. Unblinking, he sat.

It seemed as if the air around him had changed, very slightly. Had the breeze changed direction? A new awareness entered and refreshed him.

It's only me left…it's only me that can rescue Mum and Jo.

However much the responsibility paralyzed him, he had no choice. It was time to act. He slapped himself in the face, breathed in deeply and reached around to pull himself back into the house. With one foot inside, he heard the sound of breaking glass below him. Turning awkwardly, Barry lost his grip, tumbled backwards from the window ledge, and went hurtling down into the dark, savage night.

---

1. Molly had started pottery classes after going to see *Ghost* with Yamoshi. The film had given her a somewhat distorted view of the world of ceramics. After two weeks of classes in the basement of the Portslade Working Men's club under the authoritarian tutelage of a fanatical pottery taskmaster, she threw the towel in.

Chapter Sixteen

SLEEP WHEN YOU'RE DEAD

Day 4 – 3 a.m.

Barry came round on Molly's rag rug with Dr Harper crouching over him and the pungent sting of ammonia smelling salts assaulting his nose.

'How are you feeling?'

'Sore.' Barry put a hand on the back of his head.

'I thought we'd lost you there, you were lucky you landed in the hedge.'[1] The doctor opened his bag and took out a stethoscope, placing it on Barry's chest.

'They've got Mum.'

'The bastards!' spat Dr Harper. 'I hate to tell you this, but they have Merril too!'

'How do you know?'

'Quite by chance.' The doctor coughed. 'I was...going for a walk and I saw the samurai fella dragging her into a building in the old industrial estate.'

'What did you do?'

'I tried to stop him, but he almost killed me. If I hadn't thrown a vibrator in his face, he would have cut me in two!'

'Huh?'

'I'll explain later.' The doctor helped Barry to his feet, catching him again as he almost fell over.

'The room's spinning.'

'You're exhausted, boy. When did you last get some sleep?'

'Two days ago...I think.'

'Right, you need some rest.' The doctor cleared Molly's broken ornaments from the futon and lowered Barry on to it.

'There's no time,' Barry protested weakly

'Who are you going to help like this?' The doctor grabbed Barry's feet and hoisted them onto a chair in front of him.

'Make us some coffee, that will have to do.'

The doctor nodded as if he didn't have the energy to argue. He couldn't bring himself to tell Barry he had seen Jo lying motionless in that room.

Barry noticed Jo's handbag on the floor and began digging through it for her medication, sending lipstick, tobacco pouches and NHS leaflets[2] tumbling onto the carpet. Jo's scent rose up from the handbag, and he immediately pictured her smiling face. There was so much to like about her; a self-belief he could only dream of having, an impish sense of mischief, and the fact that she didn't give a fuck about what anyone else thought. Barry had been lonely for so long that he thought nothing of it, but the prospect of losing Molly, Merril *and* Jo at the same time was unbearable. Turning his back to the doctor, Barry wept big, salty tears that stung as they fell into the cuts on his arms. At last, he found a long thin plastic box marked with each day of the week and filled with pills. The label read, '*Carbamazepine*'. Barry sensed the doctor standing over him.

'You have to prepare yourself, it might be too—'

Barry clambered to his feet, holding onto the chair to steady himself. 'It's not too late, do you hear me?'

'I'm just saying, it's unlikely that—'

'It's *unlikely* that we are going to do any good here, so get your shit together.'

Barry picked up his backpack and started stuffing it with items. 'There's not a single second to lose. When we've rescued the ladies and there are three less samurai in the world, then—and only then—will I sleep. Now is the time to kill... or be killed.'[3]

---

1. This is rather curious, as there is no hedge below Molly's bedroom window. For all of you who have read the literary classic *Escape from Samsara* you may have an inkling what or rather who this might have been.

2. NHS – the National Health Service. Brits are passionate about it at the same time as telling you how the health systems in other parts of Europe are much better. In Britain, it is a system whereby people are legally obliged to pay a tax so that in the event of getting ill they can be placed on a waiting list which is six months longer than it takes for them to pop their clogs. Things are different in France though; I read about this guy called Jean Claude who died when his house collapsed on him, just outside Marseille. Five doctors from the local hospital ran to the scene of the disaster, fished him out of the rubble, and brought him back to life using re-animator cloning technology. You wouldn't get that on the NHS.

3. If you've made it this far I applaud your courage, but things start to get very messy now, so strap in. I don't know about you, but I feel that we've bonded going through this adventure together. Maybe you'd like to come round for dinner sometime? Do you like Shepherd's Pie?

Chapter Seventeen

BE CAREFUL WHAT YOU WISH FOR

Day 4 – 5.40 a.m.

H obbling down the backstreets of Portslade, Barry was careful not to be seen. Still in a lot of pain from last night's fall, he was relying on a concoction of very strong coffee and painkillers to keep him going. It was that particular time of the morning when the sun had risen but the street lights had not yet been turned off, and the only sound to be heard was the ethereal humming of electric milk floats gliding around in the background; a theatre set for a post-apocalyptic play awaiting its actors. Maybe, if you get up early enough, you have the chance to act out the way your life should have been in this surreal window of opportunity.

The doctor, knowing the most discreet routes to their intended destination, led the way; pausing behind lampposts, keeping low behind cars, and taking shortcuts through back gardens. Barry had never seen him looking so nimble. The morning frost had not yet evaporated when they arrived at the industrial estate. The doctor pulled up the collars of his coat, blew into his cupped hands, and narrowed his eyes. There was an eeriness about these husks of buildings today, as if the secrets they held were buried a little deeper and clutched to their chests a little tighter than usual, and they weren't going to give them up easily. The pair knelt wearily behind a burnt-out sofa.

'Which one, doctor?'

Dr Harper pointed sheepishly towards the shabby building at the farthest end of the estate. Its garish neon sign read '*The Pleas--e F-ctory*'; Jeffrey hadn't had the money to repair the neon for the last three years. Amid the graffiti tags on the wall below, some bright spark had sprayed '*Please Fucktory*'.

Barry stared at the sign for a few moments while his brain made some rudimentary background calculations. He turned to the doctor.

'You weren't going for a walk here at all, were you?'

The doctor shook his head timidly, picking bits of stray fluff off his tweed jacket. 'Mrs Harper would never understand...'

'Dirty bastard,' muttered Barry, reaching into his bag for his headscarf. He strapped it tight around his head and tucked his nunchucks into the front of his jeans. 'Where have they got the ladies locked up?'

The doctor fastened the buttons on his tweed coat, as if this one small detail could be the difference between winning and losing.

'Follow me.'

He scurried off, skirting the outer perimeter of the estate and bringing them out at the back of The Pleasure Factory. The doctor pointed to the small window at the back of the building that had the word '*HELP*' spattered across the inside of its grimy surface.

'Is that written in blood?' said Barry. 'For fuck's sake, I need to get in there, now!'

The doctor put his hand on Barry's shoulder. 'We need a plan. I've got the code to a secret viewing room which has its own entrance—'

'You really *are* a dirty bastard, aren't you?'

'I think I probably am,' admitted the doctor, looking quite proud of himself.

Barry gripped his arm and thrust the pill box into his hands. 'You slip in the back way.[1] Try and get Jo her medication; I'll go in through the front door and distract them.'

'That's awfully brave, my lad. Are you going to dazzle them with your ninja skills?'

Barry took his Walkman out of his bag and strapped it to his waist. 'Something like that.'

The doctor patted Barry on the shoulder, crept over to the back of the building, and punched in the magic numbers. Once he was safely inside, Barry looked in his bag for a white handkerchief and the bottle of pesticide that Brian had given him. In any other situation, Barry would sooner stick a cheese grater up his bum than take Brian's advice, but these were not normal circumstances, and Brian's words had actually made sense for once. Pulling on his kimono, Barry jogged round to the main entrance of the factory as if he didn't have a care in the world. He rang the doorbell and waited, dancing on the spot like a boxer. After a few minutes with no response, he banged hard on the glass door, waving his white handkerchief in the air.

'I'm not here to fight! I just want to talk to you. Hello?' The lock clicked, and the door swung open. Cautiously, he stepped inside.

There was no sign of life, so he walked into the main showroom. Barry's sixth sense was raging. He knew he was being watched, but *where were they?* The factory was vast.

Aisles upon aisles stacked to the brim with bizarre paraphernalia promising to satisfy every kink known to humankind stretched away into the distance. The air was thick with the most curious aromas—strawberry-flavoured love oil, edible underwear, freshly-steam-cleaned PVC, and off-gassing gimp suits. Racks of whips, chains and paddles hung from the walls. Barry could only guess at what some of the equipment was for, and he couldn't help thinking it reminded him of a shopping trip he'd taken to a military hardware store.

Sensing movement above, Barry looked up to see the three samurai stood in a line at the top of a steel staircase leading to the next level. They were immobile, staring down with Medusa eyes, their glinting swords resting by their sides.

Barry flapped open his kimono to reveal his portable cassette player, took a deep breath, and hit play. *'I'm Too Sexy'* by Right Said Fred came blaring out of the speakers, and Barry launched into some furious body-popping. A bit rusty at first, he soon began to find his mojo. His routine started with the classic two-step, progressing into the robot. As his confidence grew, he went down for a bit of floorwork. An awesome back-spin took him into a position known as the freeze which set him up for a moonwalk to the bottom of the staircase. The routine may not have won Barry first place at a New York dance-off, but it served its purpose. Above him, the samurais looked confused as hell.

Barry shouted up the stairs, 'Which one of you speaks English? I've got something important to tell you.'

The samurai with the horned hat crashed down the metal stairs in his iron boots. The sound of grinding steel echoed off the bare factory walls. He landed in front of Barry like a man-mountain, a tower of muscle and hate. Bending forward, he lifted Barry up with a single gauntlet, bringing him so close that their faces were almost touching. He spoke in a coarse gravelly growl.

'Speak. Then I keell you.'

Barry whipped out his bottle of DDT and sprayed it into the samurai's face. Dropping Barry to the floor, the warrior grabbed his eyes, screaming. Barry quickly realised this was a feigned torment, however, as the scream turned into a fiendish, chesty laugh.

'You think scented water harm *me?*' The warrior grabbed the bottle and proceeded to drink it down in one. With the other two joining in above, the samurai's laughter filled the factory. This now appeared to be a somewhat precarious situation. Barry tried to clamber to his feet and make a run for it, but the weight of the samurai's boot crashed into the middle of his back and pinned him to the floor.

The sound of snapping ribs was like firecrackers, and pain seared through every nerve in his body. Struggling to breathe, his arms splayed outward and his hands grabbed the air, looking for some kind of weapon. He took hold of a large velvety ear. Looking sideward, Barry saw Keith's saggy old face, quickly realising it was no longer irritating to find Keith staring at him in all manner of unusual places. Barry tried to speak. 'Argh...'

'You have a rather large samurai on your back,' said Keith, reaching over to the bondage display cabinet and pulling out a huge leather bullwhip with both paws. Barry lost consciousness as Keith pressed three glowing white lights on his collar to activate a static neuron oscillator, which sent a 10,000 volt charge coursing through the whip. Keith cracked it at the samurai, striking him hard in the chest. The impact hit him like a thunderclap, throwing him back and upwards and slamming him into the staircase. The samurai's horned hat rolled down the lower steps as he lay paralyzed, eyes wide open in shock. Keith knew he had to finish him off. He whipped him in exactly the same place again, causing the warrior to spring off the staircase and onto the floor below.[2]

Keith readied himself for strike number three. Lifting his whip, he was just about to deliver the final blow when a sword came circling through the air from the upper level of the factory. The blade struck Keith in the back, and he hit the floor with a dull thud. Dark maroon blood mushroomed around him. Looking over at Barry, Keith desperately tried to get his attention. Barry's eyes opened and closed as he hovered in and out of consciousness. 'Barry...I've...not got long left...wake up!' Keith kicked the whip towards Barry, and it cracked loudly with electricity as it hit the floor beside him. Barry's eyes flung open, and he grabbed his chest in agony.

'The pain—!' said Barry, gazing at Keith. 'What happened?'

'The bastards got me...it had to happen one day.'

Barry crawled over to Keith and pulled himself into a sitting position. 'You can't go, I need you.'

Wincing, Keith stared up at Barry, who could see that his eyes were struggling to focus. A single tear appeared in the corner of one of his big, droopy eyes.

'If that's your way of saying you are going to miss me...I almost feel the same. The time has come to call upon my employer.'

'Not this again.' said Barry

'Can you recall what Brian said about the legend of Mrs Jittery Twitch?'

'You mean the fairy tale? That was a joke, wasn't it?'

Keith was fighting for breath now. 'She is no fairy...and definitely... no joke.'

'He said my soul would be damned if I call her.'

'What choice...do you have?'

Barry's heart was racing as he tried to recall the chant that Brian had taught him. The two samurai on the upper floor were running down the stairs towards him.

'Do it now,' said Keith, 'before it's too late.'

'Alright, alright, I have it.'

Barry reached over and scratched Keith on his back in the spot just by his tail. With a quivering voice, he recited the incantation:

'Are you a devil? Are you a witch? Judge the soul of my enemies, Mrs Jittery Twitch.'

Looking down at Keith, Barry saw his eyes close for the last time. He held the dog's head in his arms, wondering what flavour of raw hell he had just unleashed.

---

1. The gag is there, but I'm not going to do it. It's basic and I'm above it. Just.
2. Dogs aren't into bondage as a rule, but I have to admit, it's not without its merits. I'm probably more of a giver than a receiver, though.

Chapter Eighteen

GUESS WHO'S BACK?

As soon as the incantation left Barry's mouth, the air hardened around him. His already-tender internal organs tightened, and his eardrums were sucked inward as an eerie silence swept through the building as if a nuclear launch button had been activated.

However scared Barry was, the occupants of the Pleasure Factory could not move an inch, their feet pinned down by a mysterious magnetic force. A rising temperature made it hard to breathe. Barry's throat was as dry as a desert canyon, and a coppery twang in the back of his throat made him gag as he leant forward, gasping for air.

All around Portslade, a ubiquitous sense of unease caused mothers to usher their children inside, bolting the doors behind them. The roadworks in the High Street halted abruptly due to a blown-out generator, and gangs of panic-stricken old ladies sporting curlers and hairnets flooded out of the hairdresser's when every hairdryer, curling tong, and electrical appliance stopped working in the same instant. Sparrows scattered *en masse* from the rooftops of the estate, as if privy to occult knowledge. There would be no murmuration of starlings today.

Barry's heart was a brass band inside his fractured ribcage. A strip light exploded, breaking the silence and leaving a low fizzing hum as the backdrop to this imminent festival of unknown horrors.

The Factory's doors flung open, and fog slithered in, slowly engulfing the aisles of erotic delectation. In the doorway, the outline of a figure appeared. She must have been ten feet tall, and just as wide. Sparks flew from her face as she stepped from the shadows to reveal herself – a charred, scaly hulk with fireball eyes contained by thick glasses and a face tortured by centuries spent thwarting evil. Five hundred arms rose and fell in coordinated waves, moving with perfect precision and flawless cadence. Every hand grasped a different weapon, each from a different era. All had one thing in common; they were decorated with the rotting remains of a million miscreants. Mrs Jittery Twitch had arrived.

'Hey mutha-fukkas! Guess what? Jittery's back, and I gotta tell ya, I am *pissed off*! Eight hundred fucking years of dealing with this petty bullshit! It's time for you to answer to me, douchebags, and if I don't like your answers I'm gonna suck the shit out of your ass and spit it at your momma's face. Where the fuck is Barry at?'

'Er...over here, Mrs Twitch,' said Barry, holding up his hand. 'I didn't realise you were from America.'

'I'm Jittery fukkin' Twitch, asshole, what fukkin' country did you think I was from?' Slinking over towards Barry, she stopped abruptly when she saw Keith lying on the floor.

'Who fucked up my boy?' Jittery's eyes raged incandescent, the glow spilling out from the sides of her thick black iron-framed glasses. Barry pointed over at the warriors on the staircase, red in the face from the strain of trying to break free.

'It was one of them, but I didn't see which one; I was unconscious at the time,' Barry blurted, feeling like he was standing in the headmaster's office.

'Keith has been by my side for five hundred years!' Jittery glared at the warriors. 'Today, I will deliver retribution! And smiting; you bet ya ass there's gonna be some smiting going down.' Two of Jittery's arms came forward and lifted Barry up towards her. Being at eye level with her was like standing in front of a furnace; Barry's head spun like a catherine wheel. 'You know your Limey ass will owe me for this shit, don't you?'

Barry nodded like a naughty infant.

'When I return—and return I will—you will deliver, mutha-fukka.'

'I will be prepared, muth—I mean, Mrs Twitch.'

'Let's get this party started, I gotta be in Belgium in twenty minutes.'

Interview Number One

Jittery snaked up the metal staircase, and towering over the warrior in gold-plated body armour, lifted him into the air with a solitary bloodstained hand.

'Did you kill my boy Keith?'

'No Ingleesh, no Ingleesh,' replied the samurai, shaking his head and waving his finger from side to side.

'I didn't ask what language you spoke, mutha-fukka, and it don't matter 'cause I understand every language from every era on Earth.' Sounding a little smug, she added, 'and beyond, for that matter.' Remembering herself, Jittery resumed her interrogation. 'Did you kill Keith?'

'Bad smell, bad smell.' Playing for time, the samurai pointed at one of Jittery's five hundred armpits.

'OK, homeboy, so that's how you wanna play?' Another three arms came forward to stretch him into a star shape in front of her. Jittery inhaled deeply, and her face relaxed into a serene, inward-looking expression for what seemed like an age but was no more than a few seconds. 'A judgement has been made,' she boomed as she removed her glasses and looked into the samurai's eyes.

The ensuing scream could be heard for miles around. Sludgy melted gunk that had once been a brain dribbled out of the warrior's nose and splashed onto the Factory floor, and a putrid, haunting aroma filled the building. It was the first time had Barry had smelt burning flesh. Calmly putting her glasses back on, Jittery draped the warrior over a display cabinet, where he hung like an empty fancy dress costume.

Interview Number Two

Jittery picked up the second samurai, who, despite seeing what had happened to his comrade, drew his daggers in a rather foolish show of defiance.

'Now, may I suggest we try to be a bit more agreeable?' said Jittery. 'Trust me when I tell you it's in your interests. I'm going to ask you a single question, and a yes or no is all I need to hear. Did you kill my poor defenceless Basset Hound, Keith?' One of Jittery's arms broke from the pack to point down at Keith's lifeless body.

The samurai, realising what was being asked of him, nodded his head enthusiastically. 'Yes, yes I keell, I keell. Fuk yoo.'

Shaking her head in disbelief, Jittery held him against the

wall, watching with amusement as his flailing arms tried to reach her with his daggers.

'At one time, mutha-fukkas like you had the decency to show me some respect.' With that, she took a deep breath in...and spat thousands of razor-sharp knitting needles into the samurai. This time, there was no scream, just a dull thud as the warrior hit the floor, looking like a pincushion.

Interview Number Three

Jittery's insectoid legs scurried back down the stairs towards the final warrior, who had now come round from his electric whipping ordeal. He was reciting an incantation to Sambō-Kōjin, the Japanese god of fire.

'This guy speaks English, Mrs Twitch,' said Barry, like the class tell-tale.

'Can we *please* have a two-way conversation and, if it's not too much to ask, maybe a sprinkling of respect too?'

'You look like yeti with sun-burn,' said the samurai.

'What the——?'

''I scrape dung off my boot that look like you.'

Barry laughed, quickly clearing his throat to cover it up.

'Never in eight hundred years, has anybody *ever* disrespected me like this. Prepare to be evaporated, mutha-fukka!'

'Not so fast,' said the samurai. 'First you must learn the power of Sambō-Kōjin!' The warrior stepped forward, now free of Jittery's rooting enchantment, and launching himself upward, plunged his sword straight into her heart. Every unbroken window left on the estate was shattered by her screech, as black goo oozed from her punctured, scaly skin. As her five hundred arms gathered up the samurai, cocooning and squeezing him into her body, Jittery started to quiver; a fierce ground-shaking vibration stronger than a hundred jack-hammers. Display cabinets toppled over, and chunks of plaster fell from the ceiling. Fearing what was about to occur, Barry sprinted to the back of the factory. Just then, a steel girder fell from the ceiling, narrowly missing him as he fled.

'I'll be watching you, and I *will* come calling!' Jittery shouted at the back of Barry's fast-receding head. With that, she exploded with such ferocity that the front half of the factory collapsed. Fire flared up the remaining walls as Barry found the storeroom that had been Jo's prison for the past few long days. The door was open, and Molly, Merril, and the doctor were leaning over Jo's body on the floor. Barry's heart froze. He stood in the doorway, too scared to enter.

Is it too late? Has this all been for nothing?

Molly looked up, squealed with joy and ran over, throwing her arms around him.

'Thank God! I've been shitting myself, what the hell is going on?'

'I'll tell you later, Mum.' As soon he could pry himself from Molly, Barry moved closer to Jo. To his relief, he could see she had her eyes open.

'It was touch and go for a while,' said the doctor, fiddling around in his Gladstone bag. 'She'd had a seizure, but she's back with us now.'

Jo waved Barry over and whispered softly in his ear, 'You came to rescue me.'

Barry's reply caught in his throat as an iron girder crashed down in the hallway and flames lit up the doorway.

'We're gonna be fried!' howled Merril.

'Oh no, we'll choke to death long before that,' quipped Barry, before pointing up at the small window that was now blown out. 'There—it's our only chance!'

'For fuck's sake,' said Molly. 'You're not gonna get me through that.'

'No choice, Mum. Let's get Jo out first.'

Dr Harper helped Jo to her feet. Barry leaned back against the wall, cupping his hands to hoist her upwards.

'Make sure she doesn't fall,' said Merril, reaching up to support her niece.

Jo wobbled as she scrambled to get the window open. 'I don't think I'm going to fit, it's too small.'

'Try going through at an angle,' said Barry. 'We'll push as hard as we can.'

Smoke was now flooding into the storeroom, and everyone was forced to huddle in the small area under the window. It was hard to see who was who in the thickening, acrid smog. Jo managed to get her head and arms through the opening as Barry and the doctor shoved her skywards with all their might.

'I can't keep this up much longer!' Dr Harper's knees and elbows creaked under the strain. His tears made pale streaks in the soot on his face.

'I'm stuck', said Jo. 'I can't move forwards or backwards!'

Barry tried pulling as hard as he could, but Jo cried out in pain. 'It's my boobs, they've wedged me in.'

Barry felt like a skydiver with a broken parachute.

'There's only one thing for it,' said Molly, leaning over and speaking into Barry's ear.

'No way!' Barry looked up at Jo, then back at Molly.

'What the hell are you two talking about?' demanded Jo, dangling from the window.

Molly put her hand on Jo's leg. 'I'm going out the front, darling, it's the only way to get you out.'

'You'll burn to death!' said the doctor.

'No, she won't,' said Merril, 'because I'll be with her, and that fire can fuck right off.'

Merril and Molly went over to the sink and doused themselves in water. After quickly perusing the costume racks, they chose the closest things that passed as fire protection; two leather gimp hoods.

'You ready, girl?'

Merril nodded, pulling the contraption onto her head.

'Let's run through fire.'

The duo hobbled fearlessly into the furnace of the shop floor, jumping over burning rafters in the direction they hoped was the exit. The air was saturated with a thick black smoke, making it impossible to see or breathe.

'Over there!' screamed Merril as she pointed toward a gap in the smoke. They arrived at the opening to find a burning heap of collapsed roof where the exit had once been. It was a dead end. Molly fell against Merril, coughing her lungs out.

Back in the storeroom, chunks of burning plasterboard fell from the ceiling and the doctor was buckling under the pressure of holding Jo up. 'I don't know...how...much longer I can...hold you.'

Fire was now tearing through the storeroom. The costume racks exploded into a toxic blaze, stealing the last of the room's oxygen.

'Everyone cover your mouth!' shouted Barry.

On the shop floor, Merril was desperately trying to drag Molly back to the storeroom when the collapsed roof gave way again, creating an exit out of the building. Molly clambered to her feet, having found a sudden burst of energy, and arm in arm the ladies ran into the fresh air of Portslade.

Barry and the doctor were on the verge of losing consciousness, when Jo was pulled through the window by Merril, who was balancing precariously on a dustbin. The walls of the room started to shudder, but Barry managed to scramble up behind her by using the doctor as a climbing frame. He quickly reached his hand back down for the other man, but a chunk of plasterboard came crashing down onto the doctor, sending him tumbling to the floor beneath it. The smoke had all but filled the room now, and Barry couldn't hear or see any sign of him.

'Doctor, can you hear me?' The groan of a large girder buckling told Barry that the remainder of roof was about to come down.

'Doctor, please!'

'Barry, run!' screamed Molly, helping Merril support Jo as they scrambled clear of the building.

Barry was just about to follow them when Dr Harper's hand came out of the smoke. Barry gritted his teeth and pulled with all the might left in his beaten-up body, dragging the doctor to safety just as the roof came crashing down.

Chapter Nineteen

WHIPLASH

M olly got out of bed, pulled her nightie out of her knickers, and turned the radio on.

'Yesterday, there was a catastrophic explosion in Portslade at an illegal adult sex toy factory. It is still unclear what the cause of the explosion was, but there are unconfirmed reports that it may have been started by faulty electrical wiring.'

She walked through to the kitchen, put the kettle on and poked her head into the front room.

'Come on you lot, it's almost midday. Who wants coffee?'

Barry and Jo were curled up on the futon, Merril snuggling between them like a nesting rooster.

Barry looked up from where he was lying on his back, having strapped bags of frozen peas to his ribcage. 'I'm sure they're broken.'

'I've got a fuckin' migraine,' growled Merril.

'I'll give you a rub-down, big boy,' said Jo, running her fingers through Barry's hair.

'Not with me in here you won't.'

'You can join in if you want, Ril.' Barry waggled his eyebrows.

'Mol, tell these nymphomaniacs to give it a rest!' Merril crawled out of bed and made for the kitchen, where she hoped to find sanctuary, as well as coffee and nicotine.

''Ere Mol, you know that new hairdresser, Robbie? He's only gone and asked me out on a date.'

'Really? He must be 30 years younger than you!' Molly poured coffee into four large mugs on the kitchen table.

'That's what I told him.'

'Men are supposed to go for younger women, not older!'

'I told him that too!'

'He's probably into kinky stuff, he'll be tying you up and spanking you.'

'I know, Mol.' Merril screwed up her face and fluttered her eyelashes at the same time.

Molly sat down and blew into the steam rising from her coffee. 'He's definitely a bit weird if you ask me, and he looks like Worzel Gummidge.'[1]

Merril took some lipstick out of her handbag and began smearing in onto her lips while trying to focus on a small pocket mirror. 'So anyway, I said yes, and he's taking me up the bingo on Thursday night.'

Molly fell back in her chair, roaring with laughter. 'Is that what he calls it, the dirty bugger!'

'I'm thinking of getting a boob job like Jo.' Merril pushed out her chest.

'What would Germaine Greer say?' said Barry, coming into the kitchen arm-in-arm with Jo.

'Is he a footballer?' asked Molly

''Ere, Mol, ask Barry about the lady who rescued us. She was a giant superhero cockroach who had a talking dog apparently.'

'It was the Basset Hound from next door, Mum, I told you he was looking at me funny.'

'I think you're all a bit funny,' said Molly, smiling to herself. 'Anyway, I'm not sure what I'm going to make you for breakfast, I've got nothing in and I can't be arsed to go shopping.'

Barry yanked open the bottom shelf of the freezer and produced a bumper pack of budget fish fingers, which he dumped on the kitchen table, looking very pleased with himself. With breakfast soon in the oven, Molly slipped her favourite Cradle Of Filth CD into the beat-box on top of the fridge while Merril rolled herself a ciggie. Jo grabbed Barry's hand and led him into the hallway. 'You're everything my auntie said you were and more...you've given me back some hope.' She threw her arms around him.

Barry's pulse took off like a racing whippet. He steadied himself and asked, 'So... are we gonna give it a go?'

Placing Barry's face between her hands, Jo gave him a tender kiss on the lips. Just for a moment, the pain left Barry's body.

'What are you gonna do for work now?' asked Barry.

'Well I was talking to Doctor Harper and felt inspired by how passionate he is about his job. He happily works twelve-hour days and weekends, because he knows how valuable his work is, and that is a level of job satisfaction most people could only dream of. So, I think I'm going to retrain.'

'Oh, wow. As a doctor?'

'No, a dominatrix.'

Barry didn't reply.

'I still have a list of Jeffery's customers, so I could do house calls. I think it will be very empowering. The doctor kindly said he would invest in the business.'

'He's all heart, isn't he?'

'It wouldn't bother you, would it?'

'Me? No,' Barry flapped at the air with his hand. 'I'm so

not the jealous type.' Staring down at the floor, he ground his
teeth so forcefully a filling popped out.

The pair jumped when the doorbell chimed loudly. On
answering, Barry discovered the unmistakable rosy cheeks
and top hat of none other than Bertie Backwards.

'egassem a sdnes elcaro ehT.'

'What's he on about?' asked Jo.

'He's talking backwards,' said Barry as Molly and Merril
joined the huddle in the hallway. 'I'll translate: he says he's got
a message from the Oracle.'

'This should be good,' said Molly crossing her arms.

Bertie paused for dramatic effect, his beady eyes darting
amongst his audience.

'.draziw eht eraweB'

'Beware the wizard,' said Barry.

'What wizard?' Molly frowned.

'.sesiugsid ynam htiw draziw ehT'

'The wizard with many disguises.'

'How will we know who he is?' said Merril.

'.t'now uoY'

'You won't,' said Barry.

'Well, that's useful.' Molly put on a posh accent, leaned
toward Bertie and spoke into his face, 'Do thank the Oracle
for us, won't you?' She slammed the door, and back in the
kitchen, cranked up the volume on a particularly deft bit of
shredding.

Staring at the closed door, Bertie tipped his hat and took
off down the stairs backwards. '.sdratsaB'

'I'm surprised he doesn't do himself an injury,' said Merril,
taking a deep drag on her rollie and triggering the fire alarm.

The ritual of wafting a tea towel underneath the sensor
completed, Barry found his mum in the kitchen, staring out
of the window.

'You OK, Mum?'

'I can't help thinking all this has something to do with Dad and Mindy going missing. I just don't know what.'

'I know what you mean,' said Barry. 'I promise you; I won't stop searching until I find out.'

'Right, you lot!' shouted Molly. 'Get your arses in here, we're gonna eat a bucketload of fish fingers and drink tea until it comes out our ears.'

For the time being, at least, things had returned to some semblance of normality in Portslade. The gates of the level crossing continued to beep for passing trains, the hairdresser opened his doors for what was left of the elderly community, and there was a 'For Sale' sign on the front lawn of the bowls green. In the wake of the samurai massacre, the council had been shamed into providing funding to redecorate the cinema. The roadworks continued to rumble on, and the charity shop volunteers still prided themselves on creating the most inconsistent pricing policy known to humanity. Brian was up on his allotment, drinking soup and jabbering to his onions, and Dr Harper was locked away in his garden shed, vigorously pursuing his unique and clandestine interests. Just another ordinary day in Portslade, some would say. But never forget that behind the façade of the ordinary there are unknown, unfathomed things lying in wait for their chance to appear.[2]

---

1. Worzel Gummidge – Fictional character from a children's T.V. program that ran from 1979-81. It was about a weird-looking scarecrow who comes to life and gets caught up in madcap countryside capers. He was the main reason Barry wet his bed growing up. (Don't feel bad for him; his therapist reckons in a few more years it will all be water under the bridge).

2. It looks like it's goodbye from me...it's been real. Hang on, you didn't

actually think I was dead, did you? Let's think about this for a minute. I'm an inter-dimensional Basset Hound; if you kill me in one dimension, I just get a headache in the other. This proves my dual multiverse theory, although technically each universe does have infinite permutations. At last count there were 850 billion versions of me just within our universe, but I'm pretty sure you got the best one. I'm happy to explain it further if you like...how about that dinner?

WHERE NEXT?

You got to the end...or is it the beginning? I hope you enjoyed it, and I would like to thank you for the opportunity to entertain you with the odd things that live in my head. I am getting help. I am from Brighton in England and I have a passion for writing dark comedy & sci-fi fiction.

If you would like a free copy of my dark-humoured thriller, 'A Watched Pot'. As well as updates on my future work. I warmly invite you to join my Readers List by visiting this link:

http://www.nickyblue.com/read

(I never spam or hard-sell and only email once a month)

ACKNOWLEDGMENTS

In no particular order. I owe massive thanks to all of the
following beings:
Flo: Because she's amazing. Simon Murnau: Content editing,
idea factory, moral filter and brother. Bobby J: Ideas and
sounding board guru, my comedy muse in human form.
Lauren Whale: Proof reading. Alison Gann: Feedback,
encouragement and inspiration. Chris Callard: Insight and
technical support. Natalie M Garrett: Advice and support.
Ma and Pa Blue: For encouraging me all the way. Beta
Readers: You all gave me very valuable feedback. And all my
lovely friends for listening to my nonsense.